D1178923

Bleached Bones
in the Dust

For twenty years, bounty hunter Montgomery Grant searched for Lomax Rhinehart, desperate to make him pay for an atrocity he committed during the dying days of the war.

So when Grant's friend, Wallace Sheckley, told him that he had found Lomax, Grant followed him to Sunrise, but Arnold Hays and his gunslingers were holding the town in the grip of fear. Nobody would help him and worse, Wallace had gone missing and Lomax was nowhere to be found.

With Arnold Hays the key to Grant finding out what has happened to both his friend and his enemy, he must turn to his gun to get the answers he needs. . . .

Bleached Bones in the Dust

I.J. Parnham

A Black Horse Western

ROBERT HALE · LONDON

ISBN 978-0-7090-9048-9

Robert Hale Limited
Clerkenwell House
Clerkenwell Green
London EC1R 0HT

www.halebooks.com

Typeset by
Derek Doyle & Associates, Shaw Heath
Printed and bound in Great Britain by
CPI Antony Rowe, Chippenham and Eastbourne

PROLOGUE

The bone had lain there for some time.

Wallace Sheckley knelt and poked at the rib, judging that it was the right size to be human. With his eyes now more attuned to what to look for he saw other bones dotted around in the dusty earth.

He found a long bone that had probably been a thigh, then a collection of short, squat bones that could have been a backbone, and then finally he found a skull, proving that he had come across a dead person.

The jawbone wasn't attached but he judged it as being large enough to have belonged to an adult male. Animals had scattered the remains over a wide area and so Wallace was sweating profusely by the time he'd located most of the skeleton.

He piled up the bones then sat on a boulder and supped water while he considered the remains, wondering if they helped him in his quest. He had been ten miles out of Sunrise, his destination, when a bright object had drawn him away towards an outcrop.

That thought reminded him that he'd yet to find the bright object, so he put down his water bottle and rooted through the bones again. He found scraps of clothing, but nothing that would reflect light. Then, around what he took to be a forearm, he found a gnawed length of rope.

With this discovery making his heart beat faster, he looked for wooden stakes. Feeling an odd mixture of hope and sadness he walked back and forth until, thirty feet away from the shade offered by the outcrop, he found confirmation of what had happened here.

Blown sand had almost covered them, but he kicked it aside to reveal four stakes set into the unforgiving ground in a square. Knotted rope was around each stake, the ends having been gnawed away, but the final proof of what had happened here came with the gruesome discovery of an anklebone still trapped within a loop of rotten rope.

A man had been staked out on the ground and then been left to die a lingering death.

Animals and time had removed the evidence of who this person had been in life and who had done this to him, but Wallace had a theory about the latter. And he still had the shining object to find.

He had to return to his horse to get the right angle to catch a glimpse of it again. He was pleased he'd taken the effort when the object proved to be a knife, only the tip emerging from the sand.

He gathered it up then sat on a prominent boulder to consider the scene while hefting the knife. He noted the cruel blade, the ornate hilt. He had seen this knife before.

Despite the gruesome find, when he mounted his horse he felt, for the first time in years, cheered that maybe his quest was close to an end.

There was a fort a mile away, but it appeared deserted with its stockade rotting and several of the buildings inside having been razed to the ground. So he rode on to Sunrise.

He arrived late in the afternoon at what turned out to be a substantial town with a long main drag, but which showed few signs of life and more signs of the decay he'd seen at the fort. He investigated the saloon first.

Aside from the barman only two customers were inside, leaning on the bar. They appraised him from under lowered hats, their faces hidden in the gloom. Wallace nodded to them, but got no response.

'What you want, stranger?' the barman asked.

'Coffee,' Wallace said, 'and answers to some questions.'

'I have coffee,' the barman said as he headed to the stove, the comment gathering a grunt of amusement from the other customers.

Wallace caught the hint that, as was usually the case, strangers who asked questions were unlikely to be greeted warmly.

'I want a room,' Wallace said taking the offered mug.

7

The barman nodded approvingly. 'I can provide a room if you can provide a name.'

'Wallace Sheckley.'

'And is that all you wanted to ask, Wallace Sheckley?'

'That and whether letters can be sent out from here.'

'The stage passes through once a week and gets news out. It's due tomorrow.'

'Then you've answered my questions.'

Wallace sipped his coffee. He sensed that the customers were watching him, so he turned with a smile on his lips.

'What's your business here, Wallace?' the nearest man asked.

Wallace took another sip while he considered whether to mention his quest, then nodded to himself. He put down the mug and moved along the bar to meet them.

'Lomax Rhinehart,' he said.

CHAPTER 1

Charlie Diggs wasn't as worried as he ought to be.

For the last two days Montgomery Drake had been dragging Charlie back to the law office in Mason Heights. Now he was less than an hour away from handing him over to justice.

Last month Charlie had robbed a mercantile. He'd gunned down the owner then hightailed it out of town and gone to ground.

The law couldn't find him, but Montgomery had had more luck. He knew of the Diggs brothers and their habits and so his hunch had paid off when he'd found Charlie skulking in the nearby town of Small Creek.

Montgomery reckoned the $500 reward money was worth a week's work in finding Charlie, but he had one nagging concern. For a man who was probably facing the noose Charlie was too relaxed.

Ropes trussed him up and secured him to his horse, but he rode with his head held high. He was also glancing around and this provided Montgomery with a reason for his odd behaviour.

Montgomery drew his horse to a halt, tugging back on the rope with which he'd secured Charlie's mount.

'What now?' Charlie grunted.

'We're taking a different route to town,' Montgomery said.

Charlie's eyes flared before he masked his irritation with a sneer.

'Delays don't concern me.'

Montgomery leaned forward in the saddle and smiled.

'You've got nothing to be cheered about. Get down.'

'Why should I. . . ?' Charlie trailed off when Montgomery tapped his holster. Grumbling to himself he clambered down from his mount, after which Montgomery signified that he should kneel.

Then Montgomery dismounted and paced around his prisoner. When he passed behind him he darted in and clubbed his gun butt against the back of Charlie's head.

Charlie collapsed to the ground without a sound. Montgomery kicked him over and confirmed he was out cold, then dragged him to his horse and threw him over it, letting him lie with his head dangling. When Montgomery moved on, he rode with Charlie at his side and his gun drawn and aimed at Charlie's head.

Even if he didn't intend to carry out his threat, his intent was clear to anyone planning an ambush: the first person who'd die would be the man they were trying to rescue.

Despite changing his route, two miles from town there was a ridge that Montgomery couldn't avoid without a long detour. So, from the corner of his eye, he darted his gaze between each rock along the craggy mound.

He'd all but passed the ridge when a shadow flickered on the ground beside a large boulder on the trail ahead. A moment later a man stepped out from behind the boulder but by then Montgomery had drawn his horse to a halt thirty yards back from him.

'What you want?' he asked.

'You,' the man said with a confidence that suggested he wasn't the only one involved in this attempted rescue.

'Try anything and Charlie dies.'

The man shrugged, his hand moving in a gesture that might have been to flick away a fly, but Montgomery didn't risk waiting to find out if it had a more sinister intent. He swung the gun from Charlie's form to aim at him.

The man completed the gesture by drawing a concealed gun from under his jacket, but one look at Montgomery's drawn gun made him take flight towards the safety of the boulder. He'd covered two paces and was throwing up his arms to dive for cover when Montgomery's single shot to the side sent him spinning to the ground.

Montgomery looked for movement higher up on the ridge as he spurred his horse to a gallop.

Three ill-aimed slugs whistled by his head but that let Montgomery identify where the shooters were. He turned in the saddle to pepper gunfire around that spot. The lead tore chunks from the rocks and made the shooters duck down.

Then he turned and concentrated on galloping on ahead. He passed the man he'd shot, noting he wasn't moving, then kept going.

When he'd gone 200 yards beyond the boulder he glanced back to see that four men had ambushed him. The three surviving men were scurrying to the horses they'd hobbled in a gully, but by the time they'd reached them and started their pursuit, Montgomery was a quarter-mile ahead.

As he had a substantial lead, Montgomery reckoned they'd never catch him and sure enough, after pursuing him until he was closing on the outskirts of town, they lost heart. With much surly gesturing to each other, they drew their horses to a halt and lined up to watch him ride into town, their still forms exuding a quiet menace that said this matter wouldn't end here.

Montgomery still galloped into Mason Heights, only slowing when he saw the law office, where he drew his horse to a halt.

He confirmed that his pursuers weren't visible and that Charlie was still unconscious, then tugged him from his horse. In short order he dragged his prisoner into the law office and deposited him at the feet of a delighted Sheriff Quinn.

'Charlie Diggs, I do declare,' Quinn said, tipping back his hat and giving a whooping whistle. 'He give you much trouble?'

'Nope, but some varmints thought he shouldn't end up in a cell.'

Quinn blew out his cheeks in exasperation.

'The Diggs brothers?'

'Not sure. I didn't recognize the one man I shot and the others were too far away.' Montgomery rubbed his chin as he recalled the events. 'I'll bring 'em in if it's worth my while.'

'It will be, but first, I've got something for you.' Quinn rummaged in his desk then held out a letter.

Montgomery noted the precise lettering of his name on the envelope, his eyebrows rising with interest, then took the letter from Quinn and tore it open.

He read the short message inside, finding that his old friend Wallace Sheckley had sent it, but that it had taken three weeks to find him.

'Damn,' Montgomery muttered, turning to the door.

'Wait,' Quinn said. 'We haven't discussed the Diggs brothers yet.'

'Not interested in them now.' Montgomery waved the letter.

'Important business?'

'*Old* business,' Montgomery said. Then he left the law office, his destination Sunrise.

The letter had sat propped up on the table for a week.

Although Nick Keating had looked at it every day, he had been reluctant to open it. When Walter Miller had brought out the letter, which had been delivered to his mercantile, he'd been as excited as a puppy as he waited to find out what it said.

Despite his encouragement Nick had sent him away disappointed. He didn't want to open the letter. Not when it was addressed to his father and not when his father's body was lying in the back room unburied.

But today he felt strong enough to read it. So he took the letter from the table and held it to his chest; then, in a solemn mood, he headed outside.

He walked to the tall pine that his father claimed he'd planted as a child, and lay down beside it. With the back of his head resting against the bark, he let the morning breeze cool his face before he looked at the cairn of rocks and asked the question he'd avoided asking for the last week.

'Should I open it, Pa?'

Although no answer came, he took a deep breath. Then he slit open the envelope with a finger and withdrew the single sheet of paper. There were only two sentences, written in a precise style. Nick coughed to clear a throat that had tightened, then read aloud:

14

'*Jack, I've found him. Come to Sunrise and we'll end this.*'

Nick blew out his cheeks in bemusement. He hadn't known what he'd expected to read, but it wasn't something this short and this cryptic. He looked at the pile of rocks.

'What you reckon that means?'

He waited, hoping an answer would pop into his mind. When it didn't he reread the letter, searching for details he might have missed.

Those two short sentences were the extent of the message, but scrawled at the bottom of the letter was the signature of the sender – Wallace Sheckley. Nick whistled, his interest now kindled.

'Three friends who served and fought together,' he said, 'Wallace Sheckley, Montgomery Drake and Jack Keating. You reckon I should write to Wallace to tell him you won't be coming?'

Somehow that didn't feel right.

'Then what do you want me to do, Pa?'

This time, the answer did pop into Nick's mind and for the first time in a week he felt a twinge of excitement.

CHAPTER 2

The town of Sunrise was as Montgomery Drake had expected it to be from the little he'd learnt about it, presenting a few disused buildings along with many in a state of disrepair.

It had the look of a town that was struggling to cling hold of life since the military had abandoned the nearby fort.

He drew up outside the saloon and ran his gaze along the buildings, seeing nobody about, before he headed inside. Two customers were at the bar; several more were at tables. All of them considered Montgomery, who ignored them.

'What you want, stranger?' the barman asked.

'Whiskey,' Montgomery said, leaning on the bar.

The barman provided a glass and poured a measure.

'Anything more, stranger?'

'The name's Montgomery Drake. I may be staying here a while. Where would I get a room?'

'I can provide one.' The bartender introduced himself as James Benson, then pointed upwards, signifying the room would be above the saloon.

Montgomery nodded, then hunched over his whiskey as he bided his time before he probed for answers. Wallace's message had taken a while to find him and if he had got close to Lomax Rhinehart it was likely he was long gone.

Montgomery's manhunting experience told him that the urgent need to track him down still didn't mean he needed to draw attention to himself too quickly. The first chance to press for details naturally came when one of the customers sidled along the bar towards him.

'What's your business here, Montgomery?' he asked after identifying himself as Dean Scott.

'I'm looking for a friend. I heard he came here recently.'

'Few people come to Sunrise these days. I'm sure if he came in here I'd have seen him.'

'His name's Wallace Sheckley.'

Dean looked aloft, giving the impression he was thinking back, then shook his head.

'That's an unusual name. I reckon I'd have remembered it.'

Dean was a fresh-faced youth, so Montgomery reckoned he might not come into the saloon too often.

'Then maybe he didn't have the time to give a name. Did you see anyone go through here in a hurry?'

17

Dean laughed. 'We get plenty of those, but nobody's stopped here for months.'

Montgomery resolved that he'd make discreet enquiries elsewhere later, but for now he drank up his whiskey, then asked to be shown his room.

It turned out to be the only room James let out, being sandwiched between a store and James's bedroom.

The room had a bed, a set of drawers, and a chair. It was also stifling and smelt of neglect, suggesting that Dean had been right that nobody had stayed here recently.

Montgomery dragged the chair to the window and opened it to let in a cooling breeze. Then he sat and surveyed the main drag below.

He sat quietly for an hour as the sun set and the light level dropped, but the few people he saw about didn't pay any particular attention to his room.

Then he went to the set of drawers. He dragged it away from the wall for far enough to get his arm behind, then knelt and ran his hand along the floor.

A sharp pain made him flinch back, but when he raised his hand he saw that a match that had been broken and folded at a right angle had stuck into his palm. He smiled.

'So you were here,' he said to himself, 'after all.'

He pocketed the match and went in search of sustenance. He took his horse to the stables and paid in advance for several days of fresh grain.

His generosity encouraged the owner to talk,

although he hadn't heard of Wallace. But he did direct him to Elizabeth's Eatery.

This turned out to be a clean and welcoming establishment at the opposite end of town to the saloon, where he sat alone and enjoyed a thick steak.

He talked to no one, merely looking out for anyone paying him attention. Nobody did until he paid Elizabeth.

'Nice to see some money for a change,' she said, jingling the coins and offering him a warming smile. 'You can come here again.'

'I might well do that. I'm staying above James Benson's saloon.'

'Not many do that these days.'

'I'd gathered that, but I'm looking for someone who passed through town recently. I reckon he stayed there.'

Elizabeth bit her lip while one of her two customers gave a sharp intake of breath. She considered him for longer than was necessary while finding an answer to such a simple question. Then she gave a significant glance at her customers.

'Come back when I finish up in an hour,' she whispered then turned her back on him and busied herself with clearing away his plate.

Montgomery didn't respond and left. He tried to pass an hour by making his slow way up and down the main drag, but as this confirmed that most of the buildings were derelict he found nothing with which he could occupy his time.

19

He also noted that the derelict buildings had been abandoned recently and that they had once supported extensive businesses. This observation gave him something to discuss when he returned to the saloon, but again he didn't get any useful answers.

'Things aren't going well for Sunrise,' Dean said, 'but then again it's peaceful these days.'

'Why did everyone leave?'

'The fort getting abandoned started the rot.'

'But it's not the only reason?'

Dean looked at James behind the bar then opened and closed his mouth, as if he were rejecting several answers before he replied.

'Stay here for long enough and you'll find out.'

'Then I guess I will. Sunrise was the last place Wallace headed to. Until I know where he headed to next, I won't be going nowhere.'

With that statement of intent Montgomery reverted to silence, leaving Dean and James to stew. When the hour had passed, he headed down the darkened road to Elizabeth's Eatery. No lights were on at her establishment.

He tried the door, found it closed, then peered through the window, but he could see nothing in the black interior. He stood back to consider the building.

With his eyes becoming accustomed to the dark he saw that a guarded light was casting a dim aura from a back room and so he made his way around the building.

The side was in complete darkness, so he walked slowly, feeling his way with care. He had reached the far corner when a rustling sounded behind him. He turned and peered into the darkness, but saw nothing.

Then a footfall crunched grit from the other direction.

Too late he realized the first noise had been a distraction. A sack swung down over his head and rasped down past his shoulders to his biceps.

He struggled to remove it, but his assailant wrapped his arms around him and held the sack firmly in place while pounding footfalls sounded as the other man hurried towards him. That man bundled into him, pushing him into the wall.

Unable to stop himself, he slammed face first into the wall, temporarily stunning himself and giving his assailants the opportunity to drag the sack down to his waist. Then he was pulled away from the wall and disarmed. A rope was wrapped around his waist, then drawn tight.

With his upper body constrained Montgomery delivered several wild kicks, at least one of which connected with flesh, but then the unmistakable thrust of a gun barrel jabbed into the back of his neck.

'One more kick and you're a dead man,' someone muttered in his ear.

Montgomery didn't recognize the voice as belonging to any of the people he'd spoken to so far. He straightened and stopped struggling.

21

'What you want with me?' he demanded.

'You were looking for Wallace Sheckley.'

'I was, but there was no need to attack me before telling me where he went.'

'There was. When we remove the sack, you'll know what happened to him.'

The man's tone was low and his choice of words didn't give Montgomery much hope that when he got the answer it would be one he liked, but he figured he didn't have any options. He nodded.

'Take me there, then.'

His assailants murmured to each other, questioning whether they could trust his apparent surrender, the result coming when the second man pushed him on while the first man kept the gun on him.

They moved him away from the building and back to the main drag where the light level increased but not enough for Montgomery to make out anything through the weave of the sack.

They drew him to a halt and waited. One man moved away and presently wheels trundled closer and stopped. Then he was bundled on to the back of an open wagon where his assailants pushed him to the base, forcing him to lie prone.

One man drove the wagon while the other knelt beside him with the gun still pressed against his neck.

While he bided his time until the best opportunity to escape came, Montgomery noted that they had been waiting for him. They had conducted the kidnapping quickly. And they had attempted to keep

22

him hidden.

So although everyone he had met so far had acted suspiciously, his abductors were still trying to keep their actions a secret from others in town. It was also likely that this was what had happened to Wallace and that that had made everyone be guarded with their answers.

Montgomery wasn't unduly worried about Wallace's fate yet. He was a resourceful man and he doubted that these men would have gone to the trouble of kidnapping him when it would have been easier to kill him in the darkness.

The wagon trundled out of town. Montgomery tried to take note of where they were going. It was hard to tell if they changed direction as the wagon was shaking from side to side with a natural rhythm, but he judged that this was a sign they were following a well-rutted trail.

After fifteen minutes the wagon made an obvious series of manoeuvres, then drew up. He was dragged down from the wagon, turned, then walked forward.

A hand on the back of the neck encouraged him to duck as he went through a doorway. He was walked four paces forward, then told to sit on the floor with his back to the wall.

Then one man stayed with him while the other went outside, although as he didn't hear the wagon leave he presumed he was standing guard. As it was unlikely they'd brought him here purely to let him sit in a room with a sack over his head he presumed they were waiting for someone.

This theory forced Montgomery to decide whether he should risk waiting for this man to arrive or whether he should try to escape while his assailants were still small enough in number to be overcome.

'What you waiting for?' he asked, fishing for information.

The man in the room didn't reply. Montgomery gave him long enough to say something, then carried on.

'What you want with me?' He waited again. Then, when no reply came, he continued in the same level tone, pausing between each question.

'I'm Montgomery Drake. I've come to town looking for Wallace Sheckley. Have you met him?

'Did you kidnap him too?

'I assume your not answering means you did, so why did you do it?'

This last question made the man grunt and move over to the door. He opened it and whispered something.

'Just ignore him,' the man outside said.

The man shuffled back inside, but clearly Montgomery's questions had riled him. Montgomery ran those questions through his mind, seeing nothing that should have concerned him.

Then he realized what could be worrying the man. He waited until the man was in the centre of the room, then lowered his voice, as if he were offering

24

the comment for his ears only.

'I know you.'

In truth he was only guessing that one of his captors was staying silent in case he recognized his voice, but it proved to be a good guess. The man stomped his heels, then paced back and forth, seemingly in a quandary.

Montgomery figured that his recognition of his captor's voice was a problem only if he intended to keep him alive. Feeling more confident he continued in the same low voice.

'You don't think I'm the sort of man who doesn't know what happened to Wallace, do you?' He chuckled. 'Come over here and I'll tell you what I know.'

The man continued to pace. Then, with a muttered comment to himself as if he'd made a decision, he shuffled closer.

'Tell me,' he grunted, speaking from deep in his throat in an obvious attempt to disguise his voice.

'That letter Wallace sent. You read it, but he knew you would. So he left me the important message in his hotel room.'

The man again shuffled closer to make the obvious retort.

'What message?'

This time he didn't disguise his voice as well as before and it tapped at Montgomery's thoughts. He reckoned he was one of the customers in the saloon whom Dean had spoken to briefly: Pike.

'I'll tell you later. For now I can protect you.'

'No one can. What can you do that Wallace couldn't?'

Pike moved closer, Montgomery's ferreting clearly having hit upon the right thing to say. Montgomery couldn't think what the appropriate retort was, so he mumbled under his breath.

This made Pike lean in towards him and for the first time Montgomery saw the outline of his head through the weave of the sack.

Montgomery reckoned this moment was his best chance. He braced his back, mumbled again to make Pike inch forward again, then jerked his head forward.

His forehead connected with Pike's nose with a satisfying crunch making him cry out in pain and fall backwards.

Montgomery carried his forward motion on and rolled to his feet where he kicked out, catching Pike a lucky blow that sent him rolling.

Then he stepped backwards and made the only motion he thought might remove the sack by dropping to one knee while keeping his back pressed to the wall.

The sack rode up his back and dragged out from under the rope that tied it to around his stomach. He bent double and tried to shake it away. While hearing the door opening and Pike getting to his feet, he required three shakes to remove it.

The sack hit the floor as the other guard appeared in the doorway. In desperation to buy himself a few more moments Montgomery kicked the sack, scooping it up and sending it flying into his face.

Then he turned on his heel and threw himself at Pike. The rope that had kept the sack in place had only constrained his arms rather than tying them together and so his rapid motion let him tear an arm free.

He landed on Pike's chest and sought his gun. Pike had already got it in hand, but Montgomery grabbed his wrist and squeezed. His iron grip forced Pike to drop the weapon. Then he tore out his other hand and scooped it up.

With a deft motion he slapped the gun up under Pike's chin and pressed in. Then he swirled him round to face the door. But one look at the sudden change in circumstances made the other man move away into the darkness outside.

Montgomery considered the man who was now his captive, noting he was shaking with fear. He decided that Pike was a minor cog in the plot to kidnap him and staying to question him was unlikely to provide any useful answers.

'Don't come after me,' he muttered in his ear, then he ran for the door.

Outside he saw that the other man had reached the wagon and was turning it away to escape. Montgomery chased after it, more to work off his frustration and loosen his cramped limbs than because he thought he could catch it.

After fifty yards the wagon was already a further

fifty yards ahead of him so he slowed to a halt. The driver didn't look back as he headed off into the night.

Montgomery took stock of his situation. To his left the distant dim lights emanating from Sunrise drew his attention. The wagon had gone to the right, and so Montgomery set off for town.

As he made his slow way back he considered his brief sighting of the man in the doorway, but he didn't think he'd met him before. Thoughtfully he drew the broken match he'd found in his hotel room from his pocket.

'Is this what happened to you, Wallace?' he said. 'Did you also get away?'

Montgomery hoped so, but then he registered that the match he was holding felt odd. He halted and raised it to his face, seeking stronger light.

Up close to his eyes he could see that there were two broken matches on his palm. But he had found only one match in the hotel room.

He had an ally.

CHAPTER 3

Montgomery looked down at the main drag from his hotel room, as he had done all morning.

Last night, after escaping, he had been set to storm back into town and drag out the reason why he'd been accosted from whoever got in his way. But the discovery of the extra broken match in his pocket had made him realize that more was going on in Sunrise than he was aware of, and that he needed to tread carefully.

Therefore he'd returned quietly, walked through the saloon while noting that Dean, the customer who had spoken to him the most, was still at the bar, and so was unlikely to have been involved. Then he'd gone up to his room where he had waited for whoever was behind his abduction to make the next move, but so far it hadn't come.

By early afternoon he was wondering if he should go to Elizabeth's eatery to question her when Elizabeth herself headed over to the saloon. He

29

craned his neck to watch her, seeing that she was following two men. When she disappeared from view,
he decided that this was as good a time as any to go
downstairs.

When he arrived in the saloon room Elizabeth was
standing at the bar talking with James. His arrival
silenced them both and the customers' gazes turned
to him. But after a few moments they resumed
talking, suggesting they might not have been talking
about him, after all.

This proved to be the case when Elizabeth and
James both glanced at the two new men who had
come inside. These men were propping up the opposite end of the bar. They were chortling to each other
and slapping each other on the back, acting in an
animated manner that let everyone know they were
in a good mood.

Whatever the conversation between James and
Elizabeth had been about ended and James shuffled
along the bar towards the newcomers, his slow pace
and slouched posture showing that he wasn't relishing serving them.

Montgomery slotted in beside Elizabeth at the bar.
She cast him an easy smile that suggested she didn't
know about last night's events before she returned to
watching how James fared.

'Whiskey, Leroy?' he asked.

'Sure,' one man said, breaking off from his conversation to flash James a dismissive glance. 'One for
me and one for Herman.'

James glanced at Elizabeth who gave him a nod. James returned the nod then took a deep breath and folded his arms with a determined gesture.

'Only when you've paid for the damages you caused the last time you drank here.'

His voice trailed away betraying his lack of confidence, and when Leroy broke off from his conversation to swirl round and glare at him across the bar he backed away for a pace.

'Arnold Hays's men don't pay. You need to remember that or you'll get another lesson.'

James rubbed his jaw ruefully, suggesting the nature of the previous lesson.

'I remember it, but this situation can't go on no longer. Sunrise is dying and Arnold is leeching every ounce of life out of us. If you men don't back off, there'll be nothing left.'

'Then that's what'll happen, unless you get yourself some guts.'

James gulped, then looked around the saloon, his darting eyes requesting support. The two customers drinking at a table didn't look up while Dean stayed at the bar watching their conversation with interest but with no sign of joining in. Only Elizabeth moved forward.

'He's not the only one,' she said. 'From now on if you want to eat my food, you'll pay beforehand.'

Leroy whistled under his breath while nodding.

'I might have guessed that if anyone in this god-forsaken town was still man enough to stand up to us it'd be a woman.'

'There are more than you think. You got away with not paying today, but it was for the last time.'

'So that makes two of you.' Leroy smirked as he looked around the room. 'Anyone else want to get what the others got?'

Montgomery gave Leroy enough time to enjoy the lack of a response. Then he slapped his hand on the bar with an insistent rhythm gathering everyone's attention.

'How much longer do I have to wait to get served?' he demanded.

The welcome diversion made James breathe a sigh of relief. He drew out a bottle and a glass from under the counter, bustling with obvious relish as he tried to avoid escalating the confrontation.

Montgomery clattered a handful of coins on to the counter, the noise ensuring he had everyone's attention. Then he looked around until his gaze fell on Leroy and Herman. He frowned, as if he'd noticed them for the first time, then reached over the bar and gathered up two more glasses.

With the glasses in one hand and the whiskey bottle in the other he walked down the bar past Elizabeth and Dean to stand before the newcomers, who eyed him with lively interest.

He uncorked the bottle with his teeth as he slapped the glasses on the bar. Then, with studied care he poured three equal measures.

Leroy and Herman glanced at each other and

smirked, conveying that they knew Montgomery was setting up a confrontation but that they were arrogant enough to enjoy playing along with him. They tipped their hats to him then took their whiskeys and downed them.

Montgomery ignored the third glass. They waited for him to move for it but he merely leaned on the bar.

'You not drinking with us?' Leroy asked.

'That's not for me. It's for Arnold Hays.'

'Arnold's at the fort. He doesn't come here.'

'Then tell him there's a drink waiting for him from Montgomery Drake.'

'Does he know you?'

'Nope, but I'm a friend of Wallace Sheckley.'

Leroy's eyes narrowed, suggesting he had heard of him and that his assumption that Arnold Hays was behind his disappearance might be right.

'We're not messengers, but even if we were, Arnold won't come here just to drink with you.'

'I understand.' Montgomery slowly moved for the glass. 'Arnold's too yellow to come into town, so I'd better take the drink myself.'

His fingers were brushing the glass when Leroy thrust out a hand and grabbed his wrist.

'Arnold's not yellow. He just doesn't need to come here no more now that he has us to deal with things.'

Leroy met Montgomery's eye with a surly gleam, defying him to retort.

'I've always believed you can judge a man by the

33

company he keeps,' Montgomery said levelly, 'and so if he uses worthless men like you he must be—'

Montgomery didn't get to complete his planned insult when Herman grunted with anger, then moved in on him. He drew back his fist, but before he could deliver the intended blow Montgomery tore his hand away from Leroy's grip then delivered a backhanded swipe to his face that cracked his head back.

Then he took a long pace forward and followed through with a firmer blow to the point of Herman's chin that sent him spinning away. Herman tried to grab the end of the bar to hold himself up, but his fingers closed on air and he went sprawling.

Montgomery then moved to take on Leroy, but Leroy had already prepared his next action. Before Montgomery could turn on him, he leapt on Montgomery's back, knocking him into the bar.

Then Leroy bore down on him, his weight forcing Montgomery to fold over the rim whereupon Leroy gripped his chin with one hand and a shoulder with the other hand. Then he pushed downwards seeking to grind his face into the wood.

The acrid smell of the thousands of spilt drinks that had impregnated the bar invaded Montgomery's nostrils, but with his belly pressed up against the rim he braced himself. Then he slowed his progress until his face stopped with his nose inches from the wood. Slowly Montgomery got the upper hand.

He raised himself, straining to best Leroy, while

turning. When he was almost upright he stomped round on the spot to complete a half-circle, then threw himself back against the bar, trapping Leroy between his back and the rim.

The blow made Leroy grunt. When Montgomery threw himself backwards for a second time Leroy gasped with pain.

The grip around his chin and shoulders fell away as Leroy sought to extricate himself, but Montgomery didn't give him the chance and after tensing he launched himself backwards with all his strength.

The air blasted from Leroy's chest as the movement pinned him and when Montgomery jumped forward and turned he found him swaying while struggling to stay upright. Montgomery rolled his shoulders then delivered a haymaker of a punch to his cheek that sent him spinning away to the floor.

'Had enough?' Montgomery said standing over him.

Leroy could manage only a pained groan, but Montgomery received a more strident comment from behind.

'He hasn't,' Herman said, 'but you have.'

Montgomery turned and saw that Herman had stood up. His bottom lip was bloodied and he was shaking his head as he struggled to counter the effects of the blows he'd received, but he'd gathered enough of his wits to draw his gun. Now he had it trained on Montgomery.

'There's no need to do anything I'll make you regret,' Montgomery said. 'I only want you to take a message to Arnold Hays.'

'You've gone too far for that. Arnold's orders are for us to keep the townsfolk in line. So we deal with men like you before you get ideas.'

Montgomery considered this information with a jutting jaw, then glanced at the untouched whiskey glass on the bar.

'Then I'd be obliged if I could finish my drink before we talk about it.'

'There's nothing to talk about,' Herman snapped, but Montgomery still moved away.

He stood side-on to the bar facing Herman. Then he reached for his glass with his left hand, aiming to hurl the whiskey in Herman's face while with his right hand he went for his gun. But he didn't get to complete the motion before he saw movement behind Herman in the saloon doorway. Then a new voice spoke up.

'Drop that gun or die where you stand!'

The voice was high-pitched and it sounded more nervous than the confident words suggested the speaker should be. When Herman flinched to the side he revealed a young man Montgomery hadn't seen around town before.

Herman must also have picked up on the young man's nervousness as he smirked, then settled his stance, seemingly ready to risk that he wouldn't shoot him in the back.

'I like to know the names of the men I kill,' he said.

'I'm Nick Keating,' the young man said, pushing through the batwings, 'and I don't.'

CHAPTER 4

Montgomery laughed with a confidence he didn't feel then fixed Herman with his firm gaze.

'If Nick Keating has a gun on you,' he said, 'you won't live for long enough to put a bullet in either of us. Drop that gun while you still can.'

In truth Montgomery had never heard of the newcomer, but he figured Herman wouldn't know that. Accordingly Herman darted his gaze to Montgomery and then to one side as he tried to judge exactly where Nick was standing.

Montgomery waited until his indecision was in danger of panicking him into firing, then he scooped up the whiskey glass and flung it at him. With his other hand he drew his gun, but he didn't fire when the glass hit Herman squarely on the forehead, splashing whiskey in his eyes and making him bend over rubbing at his face.

In three long paces Montgomery reached him, then used his gun hand to deliver a stinging backhanded swipe to his jaw that sent him sprawling.

A few moments later he'd disarmed Herman and was kneeling beside Leroy, checking that he didn't have any fight in him either. Only then did he look at the newcomer.

'Obliged for your help, kid,' he said. 'It's good to see that someone in town has the guts to stand up to these men.'

'I'm no kid,' Nick said, coming inside, 'and I'm not from around these parts. I came to see you.'

Montgomery narrowed his eyes as he considered the young man. A hint of recognition tapped at his thoughts and brought an unwelcome suggestion that he wasn't ready to deal with just yet. So he dragged Leroy to his feet, slapped his face to liven him up, then pointed him towards the door.

'I've asked you nicely twice,' he said, sweeping up Leroy's hat and slapping it into his stomach. 'So if you want to avoid leaving town feet first, you'll get my message to Arnold Hays.'

Leroy nodded. He put his hat on his head with a shaking hand, then made his slow way over to Herman as he attempted to leave with as much dignity as he could muster.

He dragged Herman to his feet and, as he was still stunned, Leroy had to loop an arm around his shoulders to hold him up. Then they shuffled past Nick to the door where Leroy moved round on the spot to consider him.

'You'll get his answer soon enough,' he said. 'I

hope you enjoy it before you bite the dirt.'

Leroy laughed with a mock bravado that wasn't as chilling as he'd hoped as Herman then slumped in his grasp. He had to be helped out of the saloon with his arms dangling. Montgomery watched them through the window until he was sure Leroy was taking Herman to their horses, then he nodded to Elizabeth and the barman, who returned pensive stares that acknowledged that his intervention had upped the stakes.

Only then did Montgomery feel like facing up to the news Nick would probably provide. He leaned on the bar and invited him to stand with him.

'How do you know me, kid?' he asked.

'You came to the house about ten years ago,' Nick said. 'I remember you.'

'In that case I remember you too, but you were only about this high then.' Montgomery held his hand low. 'So are you old enough to drink whiskey, kid?'

Nick bristled, but he still nodded. 'Sure am.'

Montgomery collected two fresh glasses and poured himself and Nick a measure.

'Your pa not mind?' He pushed the glass to him.

Nick frowned as he took the glass.

'He didn't.'

Montgomery sighed as Nick confirmed his worst fears.

'Did Jack get a letter from Wallace?'

'He did, but it came after. . . .' Nick's voice broke

40

and he downed the whiskey.

Montgomery poured him a refill. 'How did it happen?'

'He just went to sleep one night and didn't wake up. He hadn't been ill or anything. I thought he'd live for ever, but he didn't.'

'It comes to us all, kid, even you one day, but that's good news.'

'Good?' Nick murmured.

Montgomery nodded as he raised his glass.

'Sure. Many years ago, the last time Wallace, Jack and I were all together, we drank a toast and we all said how we wanted it to end. Jack said he wanted to go quietly sitting on his porch, surrounded by his family, a pipe in hand. It sounds as if he just about got his wish.'

Nick smiled, clearly relishing hearing a detail of his father's life he hadn't heard before.

'I hadn't thought of it that way, and I'm pleased to hear he had good friends.' He looked around. 'Is Wallace still here?'

'I don't think so, but I'll find out where he went.'

'And then what do we do?'

Montgomery noted that Nick was assuming he'd remain involved. He considered him.

'You don't know why Wallace wrote to your father, do you?'

'No.'

'Then why are you here?'

'Because if my father had unfinished business, it's

now my job to finish it.'

Montgomery smiled. 'You're Jack's son, all right, but that doesn't mean I don't owe it to Jack to refuse your offer.'

Nick firmed his jaw in a determined way that said that no matter what Montgomery said he wouldn't just turn around and go back home, but before he could speak Elizabeth came over. She glanced at James behind the bar, who gave a brief nod, then faced them.

'So you're looking for Wallace Sheckley?' she said.

'I am,' Montgomery said.

'I don't know for sure what happened to him, but I do know what he found that made him write to you.' She gave a slow gesture with a finger and thumb that mimed breaking a match in half. 'I can take you there.'

Montgomery nodded. Ten minutes later he and Elizabeth were riding out of town with Nick bringing up the rear. He had neither encouraged nor forbidden Nick from coming, but he figured they could have that debate later when he knew more.

They followed the route that Leroy and the groggy Herman had taken towards the fort. A few miles out of town they caught sight of them making their slow way onwards, but at this point Elizabeth signified that they should veer away. They headed to higher ground and when the derelict fort came into view, she stopped.

They watched the distant forms of Leroy and

Herman close on the wooden stockade. When they'd disappeared from view through the gateway she turned to Montgomery.

'That's become Arnold Hays's stronghold,' she said. 'Every few days he sends some of his men out to ensure the townsfolk aren't planning anything. Sometimes he just sends them out to cause trouble.'

'How long has he been here?' Nick asked, nudging his horse forward to join them.

'Nine months. At first he was just a thorn in everyone's rump and did nothing that the town couldn't handle, but then other gunslingers arrived and the trouble escalated. We all took sides. Some opposed him, some ignored him, some revelled in the mischief.'

'I ignore the people who accept men like Arnold,' Montgomery said. 'But I'm pleased to hear that some people in town oppose him.'

'Don't be. They're dead.' She paused to let that information sink in. 'The town banded together to run him and the gunslingers out of town, but that confrontation turned into a gunfight and then a bloodbath. When it was over ten men lay dead. Then Arnold holed up at the fort and he's been leeching the lifeblood out of the town since.'

'Then somebody needs to do something before Sunrise dies.'

She nodded. 'Some of us are planning to act.'

'And Wallace, was he another victim of Arnold's regime?'

'I don't know,' she said, looking away from the fort, her voice catching with a hint of something left unsaid. 'But I do know what he found here that brought him into town.'

She pointed towards an outcrop of rock.

'Then lead on,' Montgomery said, holding out a hand.

She nodded, then moved her horse towards the rocks. For a few minutes she searched beside the outcrop until with a cry of triumph she beckoned them over.

'Sorry,' she said. 'I've been here only once before, but this is what interested him.'

Montgomery dismounted and came over to see the pile of old bones lying almost buried in the dry, wind-blown dirt. He glanced up at Nick aiming to tell him to stay back, but Nick had already dismounted. His upper lip was curled in disgust showing that he was unwilling to come any closer.

Montgomery scraped away dirt to reveal more of the remains, but found nothing other than bones with no hint of who this person had been in life, yet Wallace had thought this discovery led to Lomax Rhinehart. Perhaps he even believed it was him.

He sat back on his haunches considering the bones, then looked up at Elizabeth.

'Anything more you can tell me?'

'I'm sorry. What you see here is all I know.' She sighed. 'I was intrigued to see them the first time. My husband disappeared a year back. There was no

44

reason for him to leave, so I reckon something bad must have happened to him, but I don't think it's him.'

'I'm sorry to hear that.'

She gulped and gave a nervous glance at the sun, as if she'd revealed something too personal.

'And whether Arnold Hays comes to town to shoot you up or not, I've spent long enough on bringing you here when I have meals to prepare.'

Montgomery thanked her for her help and walked along with her while she mounted up and prepared to leave. When she was riding back to town he paced around the remains looking for additional clues. But the bones were all that he could see.

'This might be the right time,' Nick said, 'to tell me what this is all about.'

'Why?'

'Because then I might be able to work out what you obviously can't figure out.'

Montgomery snorted. 'If I can't figure this out, you won't, kid.'

'Maybe my keener eyes will see something yours can't, old man.'

Montgomery snorted a laugh. He was still unwilling to explain the situation even though it might jog his own memory and help him to work out why these bones had fascinated Wallace.

With him not saying anything Nick shuffled around, kicking dirt from side to side as he searched.

'Give up,' Montgomery said. 'You don't know what

you're looking for.'

'Then tell me!' Nick snapped, waving his arms in exasperation.

He took a long step backwards, then moved to sweep the dirt with his feet, but his foot caught and he tripped. He fell on his back, sprawling in an undignified way that made his face redden.

Montgomery went over to him and held out a hand.

'I don't need to, kid,' he said. 'You've done a good job uncovering the answer yourself.'

Nick was about to grunt back an angry retort, but then he saw that Montgomery was smiling while looking at the object he'd tripped over: a stake that had been hammered into the ground. He let Montgomery pull him to his feet then considered it.

'I'm glad I could help, but it's just a piece of wood.'

Montgomery paced around, swishing the dirt aside with a boot until he found a second stake. Then in short order he uncovered four stakes set in a square.

He glanced at the bones judging that Wallace had probably collected them and placed them there. He moved away to sit on the nearest prominent boulder where he surveyed the scene, as he imagined Wallace would have done.

'Can you tell what happened here?' he asked.

Nick gulped. 'We can't know for sure, but it looks as if someone was staked out and left to die.'

'That's what I think, but why did this interest

46

Wallace?'

Nick didn't answer, judging correctly that Montgomery was thinking aloud. Instead, he looked at the stakes and shivered.

'It's a pity he didn't leave a clue for us to find.'

Montgomery leaned back, nodding. Despite his irritation at having gathered an unwelcome partner, he had to admit that Nick was making sensible comments.

He reached into his pocket and felt the broken matches. Wallace was a careful man who always left clues that others could pick up in case something happened to him. That thought led him to slip a hand down behind the boulder.

He rooted around in the dirt until he touched a cold object. He smiled then drew it out and held aloft what he now saw was a knife.

'He did,' he said simply.

Nick came over to consider the ornate hilt and the sharp edge that the time spent buried in the dirt hadn't dulled.

'Owned by the dead man, or by the man who staked out the unfortunate victim?'

'A shrewd question.' Montgomery considered. 'If the body is the knife's owner, Wallace would have said so.'

The first compliment Montgomery had paid him made Nick smile.

'And so that knife helped Wallace to identify the killer?'

'It did.' Montgomery tossed the knife in the air and let it turn end over end before catching it. 'And his name is Lomax Rhinehart.'

CHAPTER 5

'If Lomax Rhinehart staked out this man, then he's big trouble,' Nick said. 'So that means he'll have joined up with Arnold Hays and be helping him keep the townsfolk in line.'

Montgomery nodded as Nick again made a good assessment of where his own thoughts were heading.

'It's possible.'

Nick glanced at the bones. 'Based on what Elizabeth said, this man was probably one of the townsfolk who opposed Arnold.'

'That's also possible, and sadly it's also looking increasingly likely that Wallace proved it the hard way.'

'Then it's up to us to find Lomax using a safer way.'

Montgomery couldn't help but chuckle. 'And you say that despite having no idea who Lomax Rhinehart is?'

'If it was important to my father, it's important to me.'

'And that answer proves I can't accept your help,' Montgomery said, lowering his tone to emphasize that he was being serious.

'Why?' Nick waved his arms. 'I helped you back in Sunrise. You saw in the saloon that I can take care of myself.'

'You did help, but what I saw was a scared young man holding a gun on another man for the first time in his life and worrying about whether he had the guts to kill him.'

Nick gulped. 'Maybe, but I reckon I'd have holed him, and the second time won't be so bad.'

'It might not be, and that's why you have to leave.'

'Because I haven't faced this type of situation before?' Nick waited, but Montgomery didn't reply. 'Well, you're wrong to stop me because sooner or later I will face trouble. It might as well be at a time of my choosing.'

Montgomery shook his head. 'Nope. The problem is that a young man who's determined to fight battles he doesn't need will end up dead sooner rather than later. Wait until trouble finds you. Don't seek it out.'

'But what choice do I have? You won't explain who Lomax Rhinehart is, so all I have to go on is that my father was interested in him.'

This response made Montgomery nod and while hefting the knife with one hand he pointed at a small boulder, signifying that Nick should sit.

'You're right,' he said, softening his tone. 'I turned you down because I don't want you to get involved in something that doesn't concern you. But you have the right to decide that for yourself. So I'll do a deal with you. I'll explain who Lomax Rhinehart is, and then if that concerns you, it'll be the last we'll speak of it.'

Nick considered Montgomery's unexpected change of mind, presumably searching for traps, then sat on the boulder.

'Thank you,' he said simply, then waited for Montgomery to explain.

Montgomery continued to heft the knife as he put his thoughts in order.

'It happened twenty years ago,' he said at last, his tone thoughtful, 'in the dying days of a war that had torn apart our fine country. For three years your father had served as my lieutenant. By the time I led my company on the withdrawal across the land we'd fought to secure he'd become a trusted friend. But then I received new orders to track down a renegade bunch of Yankee raiders who'd not accepted they'd been defeated.'

Montgomery sighed as he forced his thoughts to dwell on this troubled time. He tossed the knife, catching it by the hilt. Then he threw it down in disgust.

The knife sliced into the ground and quivered before stilling.

'When do I get my chance,' Lomax Rhinehart said, his eyes gleaming with malice as he considered the knife, 'to carve myself some Yankee flesh?'

'You don't, Mr Rhinehart,' Captain Montgomery Drake said. 'Your orders are to guard the prisoners.'

'They're not prisoners. They're raiders. They stopped having rights the moment they—'

'Enough, Mr Rhinehart,' Montgomery snapped.

He stood over Lomax, ensuring that he wouldn't continue to be insubordinate. Then he gestured to Lieutenant Jack Keating to join him in checking on their prisoners before they left the camp. Together they headed into the stockade they'd erected.

'He has a point,' Jack said when Lomax was out of sight, using his role as Montgomery's closest friend to advise him on how the men were thinking. 'We saw what these men did, and they didn't have the excuse of the war.'

Montgomery nodded. 'I'm not immune from such thoughts, but nobody in my company will act on them.'

'Then I would advise that you should keep a few experienced men back with Lomax to keep him in check.'

'See to it.' Montgomery stopped in front of the circle of prisoners. 'But look at them. Who could enjoy making these wretches suffer even more?'

Jack considered the men sitting on the ground. They were scrawny and dirty. Their clothes were ragged and most had bare feet. Several were too young to grow whiskers. They all looked up at them and despite their situation they had hope in their eyes that their captors would feed them.

It had seemed so different last week when Montgomery had received his orders. Raiders had used the cover of the retreat to launch their own set of reprisals. They'd rampaged through several already ruined towns and then launched a daring attack on an army patrol that had been returning with stolen plunder.

Twenty gold bars had gone missing and Jack had been tasked with finding the men.

They'd soon found their trail and within days they'd rounded up a dozen of the raiders, all of whom had given up without a fight, but six men remained at large.

The prisoners had refused to talk about the free men or the gold, so Montgomery had decided to leave behind a detail to guard them at their hastily erected camp while he tracked down the rest.

Jack turned away then pointed at Lomax, who was lurking at the entrance to the stockade eyeing the prisoners with unconcealed malevolence. He had now picked up the knife he'd claimed from one of the raiders and was sharpening it on a stone.

'You're right,' Jack said. 'None of the men would have the stomach to take out their anger on captured men, except one.'

'There are men under my command,' Montgomery said, his tone tired, 'who relish war but have no place in a time of peace.'

'And then there are men who were competent in

peacetime but have no place in a war. I've always pre-
ferred that type.'

Montgomery nodded. Recently their thoughts had
often turned to the forthcoming adjustment to a new
life. Montgomery had no idea what he wanted to do
in the future while Jack was thinking of staying on in
the military. The rest of the company all worried
about whether they could fit back into the lives
they'd led before.

For some men that transition would be hard. And
for a sadist like Lomax Rhinehart, who had been a
vital member of the company in battle, Montgomery
didn't feel any sympathy for the difficulties he'd face
in returning to normal life.

With the discussion over, Montgomery gathered
his men and they moved out to pursue the remaining
raiders.

As it turned out, the battle to capture them was
even easier than the battle to round up the original
group. They tracked them down to an abandoned
barn sitting beside a torched farmhouse.

Five of the six men were already dead. The last
man breathed his last shortly after they arrived. None
of them had died from battle, but from the other bat-
tlefield killer: sickness caused by hunger and
wallowing in human filth. The barn stank of disease,
so Montgomery gave the order to keep the dead men
in the barn and torch it.

Of the gold there was no sign, but then again
Montgomery had expected this to be a likely conclu-

sion to their search. For several years confusion and misunderstandings had been his constant companions and he had always doubted the story that the men were fleeing with such a huge stash of gold.

They returned to camp to pick up their captives. On the way everyone was content despite the grim ending to their search. This was their last duty and unless more orders arrived, they could make the long journey home now.

The first hint that this journey would be delayed came as they approached the camp. Nobody was standing guard and even with the recent incvitable slackening of discipline this was unthinkable. Montgomery sent two men on ahead to find out what had happened.

Both men rode into the camp looking around. One man investigated the tent where the men slept while the other went into the stockade. He came out bent over then vomited on the ground.

The man was a hardened veteran who'd seen many terrible sights in the last few years, so when Montgomery investigated he did so with trepidation. The buzz of flies was the first hint of what lay ahead and when he looked into the stockade he too felt bile rise in his throat, even though his worst fears hadn't materialized.

His men weren't here. The dead men were the prisoners. The manner of their deaths though was beyond anything he'd seen during his years of warfare.

At the compass points around the stockade four men had been pinned up, their fly-blown guts spilled to the ground. Their deaths had probably been preferable to that suffered by the other eight men who had been staked out on the ground.

Montgomery examined only the first but that was enough to confirm these men hadn't died easily. He turned away and called out for a burial detail to give them the dignity in death they'd been denied while they'd still clung on to life.

Jack met him at the entrance and Montgomery summed up the situation with a single comment.

'Lomax Rhinehart,' he muttered.

'It has to be, but what about the others? He could-n't have persuaded a senior officer to go along with such brutality.'

'He shouldn't have, but maybe I misjudged them. Twenty gold bars is a terrible temptation for hungry men.'

'We both made that mistake,' Jack said.

Montgomery patted his shoulder acknowledging that he welcomed his friendship but that the respon-sibility was his.

Within the hour the weary soldiers left the aban-doned camp for their most onerous duty so far: of tracking down their own men.

This time their quarries were resourceful. They led them on a circuitous chase across a blasted land-scape, but Montgomery's strategic sense defeated them. He worked out where they were going.

No matter in which direction their quarries headed they always stayed close to the burnt-out farm where they'd found the last of the raiders. So they holed up there.

Montgomery settled down beside the derelict barn. As had often been his wont when making a stand, he thrust his sword into the ground. Then he waited for the renegades to come to them.

Within a day they rode into view and then, on finding that they'd been outmanoeuvred, they gave up without a fight, but only five of the original six men had come. Lomax Rhinehart had already left the group.

When Montgomery received that information he withdrew the sword and held it aloft. . . .

He considered the blade. Then he looked at Nick.

'And that's why we want Lomax Rhinehart,' he said.

'He's an evil man.' Nick bit his lip, clearly unwilling to voice the thoughts that must have occurred to him while listening to the tale. 'But I can see why you don't want me to help you. It doesn't seem to have anything to do with me.'

'It doesn't. Men die in war, and even if this was something different, they all suffered long before you were even born.'

Nick nodded and when he spoke his voice was resigned, as if he had already decided that he would turn away from this quest.

'In that case why does it concern you? The men who were killed died horribly, but they were raiders and they were on the other side.'

'They were.' Montgomery sighed, wondering whether he should complete the story now that Nick was talking himself round to leaving, but he figured he deserved a full answer. 'But that didn't end the matter. In war, rumours spread faster than wildfire, but when they contain an element of truth the results can be explosive. Other prisoners thought they'd be killed too, so they escaped and rebelled. In one night I lost more men than in the previous year.'

'And that's the reason for this quest?' Nick watched Montgomery nod, then thoughtfully stroked his chin. 'And it wouldn't have helped my father's career. He had wanted to stay on in the military, but that must be what stopped him.'

Montgomery smiled. 'It did, but don't go thinking like that. You only exist because he didn't pursue that life.'

Nick took the opportunity to lighten the mood and laughed.

'Maybe, but I'm starting to think this does concern me.' He considered. 'And where does Wallace Sheckley fit into this?'

'In some ways he suffered the most. Wallace was the second lieutenant I left in charge of the prisoners. He tried to stop Lomax, but he couldn't. Afterwards, nobody listened to his excuses. He got ten years in jail. When he came out he vowed to kill

Lomax. He's been searching for him ever since.'

'Then I'll join him and you.'

Montgomery took a deep breath, wondering if there was anything he could say to change the young man's mind, but he had promised he would let Nick make his own decision.

'Then you're welcome. And I hope our partnership lasts beyond sundown.'

With that thought they turned away from the remains and headed back to their horses. They'd reached the trail at the point where they'd first left it when Nick asked the question Montgomery had expected him to ask earlier.

'What happened to the gold?'

Montgomery shrugged. 'Everyone thought Lomax had sneaked away because he knew where it was and he wanted it for himself, but nobody knew for sure. Nobody ever found it either, so maybe he did get it. Or maybe there never was any missing gold. I'll be sure to ask him before I kill him.'

'Provided we don't get shot up by Arnold Hays first.'

'We won't be. I didn't annoy Herman and Leroy because I have a death wish. There are people in town who will face up to Arnold. They just need encouragement.'

'Then you'd better provide that encouragement quickly.'

Montgomery was about to ask what he meant when he saw that Nick was looking back along the trail towards the fort.

He followed Nick's gaze. Around a dozen men were coming out through the gateway. The sunlight twinkled off their amassed weaponry as they speeded to a fast trot.

CHAPTER 6

Montgomery drew up his horse outside the saloon.

'Find Elizabeth,' he said to Nick while pointing down the road, 'and tell her what's happened. I'll talk to the ones in here.'

Nick nodded and after a worried glance out of town, he hurried off. Montgomery couldn't help but glance back along the trail too, but the following men weren't visible yet, and so he still had time to persuade the townsfolk to join him in making a stand against Arnold Hays.

He went inside. With sundown an hour away the saloon had more customers than earlier. Montgomery wasted no time in heading to the bar where he grabbed a glass and banged it down with an insistent rhythm.

'Arnold Hays is coming,' he said simply.

'Ten men died the last time,' Dean said, shaking his head. He downed his drink and quickly poured another.

'And ten men might die again today,' Montgomery said, 'but if we band together we can make sure that this time it's the right ones who die.'

Everyone glanced at each other with shamefaced looks that suggested they were wondering who would risk arguing with him. None of them met his eye.

Dean snorted. 'We saw what happened here earlier. You're the only one who wants to take on Arnold Hays. So this is your battle.'

Supportive muttering echoed around the saloon.

Montgomery sought out each person who was agreeing with Dean and glared at him until he quietened. Only when silence had returned did he speak, choosing his words carefully as this would probably be his last chance to persuade anyone to join him.

'This town is dead and so are you, except you haven't realized it yet because you think that just because you can fry your brains with gut-rotting whiskey then you're alive. But you're wrong. This town died when you let Arnold Hays take over and it won't live again until you stand up to him.'

For the first time several men murmured in a supportive way, but most still shook their heads.

'Don't malign the men who died supporting this town,' Dean said. 'We did the best we could, except it wasn't good enough. That was our only chance. We lost it. We accept we're dead now.'

'If you're dead, then what have you got to lose by trying to live again?'

Dean lowered his head as did the men who had offered mild support. The rest waved dismissive hands at him. Silence reigned for several seconds until a new voice spoke up from the doorway.

'Nothing is what we've got to lose,' Elizabeth said. 'Because the only ones taking a risk here are Montgomery and Nick.'

Montgomery swirled round to face her.

'Obliged for your support,' he said.

Elizabeth came into the saloon while Nick stayed outside to look down the road for Arnold.

'Arnold's still not in sight so there's time to act.' She turned to James, then slowly cast her gaze on to Dean, then the rest of the customers. 'We've talked about mounting another assault for a while now.'

'We have,' Dean said. 'But our plans aren't ready yet.'

'We were waiting for the perfect time to act, but maybe that time will never come.' She gestured at Montgomery. 'And now a new man's in town and he already has a plan to defeat Arnold, don't you?'

'I do,' Montgomery said cautiously, noting the significant glance she was shooting at him.

'And for it to work,' Elizabeth said quickly before anyone picked up on his uncertainty, 'he needs to know you'll follow what he's started.'

Stronger supportive comments started up.

'But we haven't worked out all the details,' James said, although his tone sounded more enthused.

'And we never will if we just talk,' Elizabeth said.

'Getting Arnold out of the fort has been impossible, but now Montgomery's enticed him here. So I say this is our only chance and we have to seize it.'

'And if we fail?' Dean asked.

'If we back Montgomery's plan, we won't.' She stared at Dean until he pushed his drink away untouched. This statement of intent made several men stand. 'And remember he's taking all the risks in getting Arnold. We just need to follow his lead and do our part.'

More men stood. Then they looked at the ones who were still seated and they started to argue that they should join them.

With nobody paying him any attention, Montgomery moved over to join Elizabeth.

'Before Arnold rides into town,' he whispered from the corner of his mouth, 'I'd be obliged if you'd tell me what my plan is.'

Arnold Hays drew his horse to a halt in the centre of the road with his men lined up on either side.

'I've come for Montgomery Drake,' he proclaimed, his voice echoing in the otherwise deserted road.

In the abandoned hotel opposite the saloon Montgomery gestured at Elizabeth to stand back from the door. Then he ran his gaze along the gathered men.

They had their hats drawn down low, shrouding their features in shadow. Although, with it being

64

twenty years since he'd last seen Lomax Rhinehart, he was unsure whether he would recognize him.

'Are these all his men?' he asked.

'I'm not sure,' Elizabeth said, peering past Montgomery at the dozen riders. 'But I think more than this are at the fort.'

This sounded likely. Lomax Rhinehart had thrived in doing his evil business in the shadows while letting others take the risks.

Montgomery stood tall and walked out into the road. The gazes of the line of riders turned to him. Herman was sitting beside Arnold and he identified him, the observation making several men edge hands towards holsters while the rest maintained their studious consideration of the buildings.

'I'm the man you've come to meet,' Montgomery said swinging to a halt in the centre of the road.

Arnold leaned forward in the saddle to look down at him, his narrowed eyes showing he expected deception, but with the odds being so heavily stacked in his favour, he had a confident demeanour.

'State your business,' he said. 'Then I'll kill you.'

Montgomery looked along the line of riders. From his new position he could see their faces, but none of them resembled what he thought Lomax would now look like. He gestured to the hotel.

'My proposition is for your ears only.'

Arnold shook his head. 'I don't work that way. Whatever you have to say, say it here.'

Herman and Leroy grunted their approval and

the conversation gathered the interest of the rest of the riders as they accepted that trouble from the townsfolk was unlikely.

'Then I'll tell you what I want.' Montgomery raised his voice. 'Give me Lomax Rhinehart.'

Arnold furrowed his brow with momentary bemusement while Herman and Leroy glanced at each other.

'That's a bizarre request, but if I were to give you Lomax Rhinehart, what do I get in return?'

This was the key moment on which the success of the trap rested. If he couldn't entice Arnold to move away from his men, it would be difficult to sow discord and it was likely that the reticent townsfolk wouldn't join him.

Unfortunately he had nothing to offer. So he merely raised his jacket to show he was unarmed then turned on the spot while patting his jacket to convey he didn't have a concealed weapon. Then he gave a significant look at the abandoned hotel and set off towards it.

He walked slowly, reckoning that he had played his hand and if he were to make any further attempts to get Arnold to follow him that would make him even more determined not to. He'd reached the board-walk when an irritated grunt sounded. Then hoofs clopped behind him.

He didn't react as, within the open doorway, Elizabeth came into view and nodded, confirming that Dean and Nick were now in position before she disappeared into the shadows.

Montgomery paced up on to the boardwalk then turned to see that Arnold had moved away from the line of men and was cautiously riding towards him.

'I can give you a future beyond Sunrise,' Montgomery said while Arnold was still moving on, showing that he wasn't trying to get him to come into the hotel.

Accordingly Arnold drew his horse to a halt in front of the boardwalk where he peered down at him, as he was supposed to do.

'What future?' Arnold grunted.

Montgomery delayed his response by rubbing his chin as if he were pondering. Then he slipped his hand into his jacket. He moved slowly to show he wasn't planning to withdraw a weapon.

Arnold moved his horse on a half-pace. This movement placed him within range of the trap, so Montgomery raised his voice.

'I can get you anything you want.'

Arnold waited for him to explain, but then Herman uttered a cry of warning. Arnold flinched, then looked up as a shadow flitted over his form. A moment later the net thrown by Dean and Nick from the hotel roof landed over him.

The weights at the corners dragged the net down to a few feet from ground level. His spooked horse sprang, tearing holes in the net but also unseating him. He fell entangled and hit the ground, landing on his side, then he was dragged along by his mount for several yards until the horse shook the net loose.

Then the shooting started.

It exploded out from the saloon doorway and from the windows as the customers carried through with their promise to take on the riders. But Arnold's men reacted instantly and peppered gunfire at the saloon, smashing glass and sending the figures scurrying into hiding.

Montgomery put their battle from his mind and concentrated on completing his part of the plan. He hurried out into the road with his head down.

As from the corner of his eye he saw several riders turn their guns on him, he dived to the ground and slid to a halt beside Arnold. He grabbed him within his confining net and dragged him to his chest to use him as a shield, making the riders stay their fire.

'You've made a big mistake,' Arnold muttered while struggling to free himself.

'The only mistake made was yours. I only want Lomax Rhinehart.' Montgomery dragged him to his feet. 'Call off your men and we'll talk this through.'

'No deal. You're a dead man no matter what you do now.'

Montgomery didn't know whether Arnold was merely acting in a tough manner, but he postponed worrying about it until he had gained the safety of the hotel. Walking sideways he paced up on to the boardwalk and then through the doorway to join Elizabeth.

She passed him his gun then turned her own gun

on the netted Arnold. Montgomery pushed Arnold to a sitting position at the bottom of the stairs, then peered through the doorway.

Gunfire continued to rip out, but mainly from Arnold's men. The townsfolk in the saloon were keeping down and the others who were supposed to be launching an attack from the stables weren't making an obvious attempt to join in the assault.

Only Dean and Nick on the roof were succeeding in their roles by keeping Arnold's men pinned down. Most of them had dismounted and had scurried into hiding outside the abandoned mercantile beside the hotel. They were risking moving out to shoot upwards, then scurrying back into hiding when Nick and Dean returned fire.

A few men had remained mounted. They'd congregated beside the saloon, taking advantage of being out of easy range from the roof while training their guns on the saloon and stables as they waited for anyone to risk showing themselves.

So far there had been no casualties on either side, but that situation couldn't continue for long as sporadic gunfire continued to blast down from the roof. Montgomery joined in the shooting by poking out through the doorway and firing at the nearest men.

They soon realized that gunfire was coming from a new direction and two men bobbed up and splayed lead at him. Montgomery darted back as the slugs whined through the open doorway and kicked splinters from the side of the door.

He waited for a lull, then risked looking out. Leroy was making a run for the door. Behind him the other men had got themselves organized.

Several men had slipped out into the road to take pot shots at the roof while two others covered Leroy. Slugs whined on either side of his running form as the men concentrated on forcing Montgomery to retreat.

When one shot clipped past his arm, fraying cotton, Montgomery jerked back out of view. He pressed his back to the wall as Leroy's footfalls pounded across the boardwalk. He stomped to a halt on the other side of the wall beside the door.

'Give him up, Montgomery,' Leroy demanded.

'He's staying with me,' Montgomery said, 'until you men agree to throw down your guns.'

Leroy snorted, but then a murmured command came from some distance away. A bang on the wall sounded, giving Montgomery the impression Leroy was gesturing. Then Leroy spoke up.

'All right,' he said, 'I'll come in and discuss this.'

Leroy's sneering tone gave Montgomery no doubt that he was planning deception, but he figured he didn't have a choice.

'Come in, then,' Montgomery said.

CHAPTER 7

'We've pinned them down,' Nick said, peering over the top of the false front and seeing Leroy disappear from view, 'but that's all we can do unless more join in.'

Dean nodded. 'They will do, and don't be hard on them. We've had so many setbacks, it's not surprising they haven't committed themselves yet.'

Nick winced, this comment confirming his worst fears.

'Then what do they need to see to make that commitment?'

Dean loosed off a shot down at the mercantile, then turned to Nick, his firm jaw showing he was giving the question serious consideration.

'We need to show we can prevail. Then everyone will throw everything they can behind this assault.'

Dean opened his mouth to continue speaking but then bit his bottom lip as if there was something more he had thought of saying. Nick considered him, wondering how he could get him to talk, but then he settled for an alternative approach.

'How old are you?' he asked.

Dean moved away from considering the scene below, his eyebrows raised in surprise.

'I'm eighteen.' He rubbed his jaw. 'Or at least I think I am.'

Nick flinched back in surprise. 'I didn't realize we're the same age. You look older.'

'I feel it. But I guess you've had a more comfortable life than I have.'

'I guess I have.' Nick pointed down at the road below. 'But maybe we can make it easier from now on.'

'And I'm obliged for your help, but talking won't get this finished.' Dean then set about laying down gunfire at the mercantile.

Nick joined him and for the next minute they stopped the men outside the mercantile from venturing out and returning gunfire. They did so well that the other group of men outside the saloon concentrated their efforts on them.

Still on horseback one man took pot shots at them, but luckily the lead all flew wide, whistling overhead or slamming into the hotel wall.

Nick decided to respond to their assault and while Dean concentrated on the mercantile he fired at the group in the open. His shots were also wild, but with the men having no cover he stood a greater chance of getting lucky than they had of hitting him.

72

The men accepted they were vulnerable. They jumped down from their horses and while one man covered them they ran to the saloon.

Dean's interested grunt showed he'd noted the change of tactics and that this could be the crucial moment in the gunfight. He joined Nick in splaying gunfire at them.

Their shots clattered into the saloon wall, but the wild volley helped them to judge the distance and their second volley came closer. One shot even pinged into the boardwalk a few inches from one man's boot.

Acting hastily two men hunkered down on either side of the door. They glanced at each other to co-ordinate their attack. Then they charged inside.

Nick and Dean loosed off shots at their backs before they disappeared from view. Then they aimed to pick off the men who were still outside while the battle for control of the saloon got under way.

They'd managed only a couple of wild shots before one of the men who had gone inside appeared at the door. Lying on his chest and with his elbows planted firmly beneath the batwings he fired up at them.

Lead tore into the wall a few feet to Nick's side and the next shot sprayed splinters in his face forcing him to duck. He glanced at Dean to see he'd done the same.

'They took the saloon easily,' Nick said.

'They sure did,' Dean said, shaking his head. He

bobbed up to look at the saloon, then ducked down as another shot whined past his head. 'I'd have expected James and the rest to at least put up a proper fight.'

'If they've lost heart, we need to prove to them that they can win through.'

Nick stared at Dean until he nodded. Then he bobbed up and with gritted teeth he fired at the saloon. Now both men who had gone inside had appeared in the doorway and the other men had gone to ground in an alley beside the saloon.

With few targets to aim at he shot only once more then ducked down to reload. He punched in bullets with speed, but then from the corner of his eye he saw that Dean had moved from his previous position.

He had started to turn to see where he'd gone when cold steel pressed into the back of his neck.

'I'm sorry,' Dean whispered in his ear. 'It's over.'

Leroy edged into view through the doorway with his hands held high and his gun aimed at the roof. He considered Elizabeth who was still holding the entangled Arnold at gunpoint at the base of the stairs. Then he faced Montgomery.

'Drop the gun and we can talk,' Montgomery said.

Leroy shrugged then opened his hand to let the gun fall to the floor.

'Now lower your gun and we can talk,' he said.

The lively gleam in Leroy's eye suggested that his apparent surrender was a prelude to duplicity, so

Montgomery paced backwards to the base of the stairs.

'Join Arnold and then the rest can negotiate for your release.'

'You've double-crossed me,' Leroy muttered, standing his ground.

For long moments nobody moved. Then Arnold spoke up.

'Do as he says, Leroy. Give him his moment of triumph.'

Leroy brightened, then nodded. As he slowly walked towards Arnold footfalls sounded at the top of the stairs. Nick and Dean were the only people up there, but they shouldn't have come down yet when they were commanding such an advantageous position.

Then Montgomery noted that the gunfire outside had petered out. He moved to bring the top of the stairs into view, but before he could see who was coming down, Leroy took that as his chance to attack him and he threw himself forward.

Leroy had managed two paces and was thrusting his arms up ready to leap at him when Montgomery turned at the hip and blasted a low shot into his guts that made him fold. Leroy ran on for another stumbling pace, his hands clawing at his holed stomach, before he ploughed headfirst into the stairs where he lay, twitched, then stilled.

Arnold looked down at the body with an unconcerned air then pointed up the stairs.

Montgomery turned. To his surprise Nick was coming down the stairs with a resigned tread and his hands raised. Dean was following on behind with his gun trained on his back.

'You turned on us,' Montgomery muttered.

'I didn't,' Dean said. 'We were never going to win this battle.'

'We had them pinned down. James only needed to organize everyone in the saloon and—'

'James would never do that,' Arnold said. 'Now drop that gun, Montgomery, or your young friend dies.'

Montgomery looked at Elizabeth for support, but with a shamefaced shrug she lowered her gun. Despite the lack of support he reckoned he could probably shoot Dean before he managed to loose off a shot, but then he heard footfalls behind him. He hadn't known that anyone else was in the hotel.

Still keeping his gun drawn, he glanced to the side. Two men were emerging from the darkened recesses of the hotel with their guns drawn. And he'd seen them before.

They were the men who had tried to kidnap him last night.

Accepting that he was outgunned, Montgomery dropped his gun to the floor. Then he raised his hands as Pike, who still had a red nose from last night's head butt, frisked him for weapons.

Pike smiled when he came across the knife he'd found at the outcrop. He tossed it to Dean, who used it to cut through the netting that still entrapped Arnold. Then he moved on to frisk Nick.

'Sorry,' Nick whispered from the corner of his mouth. 'I didn't expect them to turn on us.'

'Neither did I,' Montgomery said.

He glared at Elizabeth, still unwilling to accept she had joined in the duplicity, but she wouldn't meet his eye. Dean wouldn't look at him either. But when they looked at each other Elizabeth gnawed on her lip while Dean gave a resigned shrug.

Clearly more was going on here than just Dean having double-crossed them. But Montgomery didn't get a chance to gather any clues as to what was happening when Pike's accomplice – identified as Snyder from Pike's grunted order to approach – moved in and dragged a sack down over his head. Nick received the same treatment.

'Two this time?' Pike asked.

'As I promised,' Arnold said.

'Then we pick these two.'

'As you wish.'

Then, in a repeat of last night's abduction, Snyder walked him out of the hotel and into the road. He and Nick were told to stop.

In short order a wagon drew up and Snyder bundled them into the back. Pike sat them down behind the driver's seat, then tied rope around their ankles to secure them to each other and to the wagon.

Snyder headed the wagon out of town while Pike

77

sat in the back with them. Over the trundling of the wheels Montgomery heard Arnold issuing orders to search the saloon and to quell any rebellion with hot lead, but gradually the sounds of commotion receded.

Montgomery again tried to note the direction they were heading. He judged they were broadly heading in the same direction as they'd gone last night, but he also reckoned they were going uphill. And the wagon shook more than the previous time suggesting they were heading over rough terrain.

'Stop thinking of escape,' Pike said.

'I wasn't,' Montgomery said.

Pike snorted a harsh laugh. 'You ought to be. Last night you got away. This time you won't avoid your fate.'

CHAPTER 8

On the back of the rocking wagon Montgomery bided his time.

Last night he had merely been abducted, and despite the threats Arnold hadn't made it clear that they were being taken away to be killed.

Nick had said nothing. He was sitting upright beside him and knocking against his side whenever the wagon went over a rut.

He had impressed Montgomery. Despite his initial misgivings Nick had conducted himself in a way that reminded him of his father in his younger days. He therefore had no doubt that if an opportunity to escape came their way he would do the right thing to help him.

What he didn't expect was that Nick would be the one who provided the opportunity. Using the cover of the rocking wagon to disguise his motion, Nick fell against him.

'I know where we are,' he whispered. 'The moment

they try to get us out of the wagon, follow my lead.'

Montgomery tried to use the rocking rhythm to knock against him and ask for more details, but Pike spoke up.

'Be quiet,' he muttered. 'You'll get plenty of chances to make noise soon enough.'

'What does that mean?' Montgomery said, hoping to goad him into revealing more, but Pike didn't reply.

Then the wagon creaked as Pike raised himself to look ahead. Montgomery discovered the reason why when Snyder turned the wagon in a part-circle, then drew it to a halt.

'Get up! he demanded.

Montgomery moved to rise, but then sensed that Nick had stiffened. Reckoning this was the moment that Nick had planned to put his escape idea into motion he sat back down.

'We're going nowhere,' Nick said.

Pike grunted with irritation. He told Snyder to help him and the wagon creaked as he jumped down.

As Snyder came round to the back, Pike rolled to his feet and came towards them, his form just discernible through the weave of the sack. He thrust out an arm aiming to drag Nick to his feet, but Nick kicked out and the sound of a heavy thud proved he'd knocked Pike off his feet.

Montgomery struggled to remove the sack before joining in the fray, but Nick barked out an order as he too tried the tear his sack away.

'I'll deal with him,' he said. 'Get us out of here.'

Montgomery jumped to his feet and ripped the sack from his head. He saw that they'd stopped beside the outcrop of rock he'd visited earlier that day, except they were a mile further along it and closer to the fort.

Snyder was moving to climb on to the back of the wagon. Herman had accompanied them on horseback and he was riding round to the other side of the wagon to cut them off if they ran. But Montgomery had no intention of doing that. He and Nick were tied at the ankles to the side-boards and it would take too long to get free, so instead he stepped over into the driver's seat.

This moved him to the limit of the leeway he had with the rope forcing him to sit in an ungainly manner with the constrained leg thrust to the side and resting on the back of the seat. That didn't stop him reaching the reins and with a snap of the wrist he encouraged the two horses to move off.

On the back of the wagon Nick and Pike were still fighting while Snyder struggled to climb on board the moving wagon. Heartened, Montgomery yelled at the horses while hurrying them on. The extra speed encouraged Nick who dragged himself away from Pike and stood up.

He teetered as he gained his balance, then he grabbed Pike's collar and drew him to his feet. With his feet placed wide apart he steadied himself to deliver a round-arm punch to Pike's jaw that sent him reeling to the side of the wagon. Pike made to grab the side-board, but his momentum was too great and he went flying over the side.

'Good punch, kid,' Montgomery shouting while beckoning. 'Now get up here and get this rope off me.'

Nick waited to ensure that Snyder wouldn't clamber on to the wagon, but it was now moving quickly. Snyder was sprinting, but he was struggling to keep pace, wheeling his arms as he sought extra pace. For his part Pike got to his feet but on seeing the lead the wagon had he merely kicked at the dirt in irritation, then slapped his hat to the ground.

With a smile on his lips Nick rolled over on to the front seat. Like Montgomery he had to sit sideways and place his foot on the back of the seat. But without the reins to worry about he was able to work on the knots to free himself.

While he tugged he cast glances at Herman, who was the only one likely to stop them. Now he'd drawn level with the back of the wagon and was moving alongside.

'Give up,' he shouted.

They both ignored him as with a cry of triumph Nick freed his leg. That lessened the tension on the rope holding Montgomery and let him lower his leg to a more comfortable position.

He passed the reins to Nick and moved to free himself. Then from the corner of his eye he saw

Herman was matching the speed of the wagon. In a reckless move Herman stood tall in the saddle and launched himself over the gap to slam into Montgomery's side.

The force sent Montgomery skidding along the seat, only the rope he had been trying to remove saving him from being sent crashing to the ground. He lay on his back gathering his senses then moved to right himself. Before he was able to tussle with Herman, Nick barged past him and grabbed his assailant.

With Nick having released the reins Montgomery reached for them. He concentrated on steering a steady course as Nick inexorably forced Herman to the edge of the seat.

His progress was so assured that Herman cast a worried glance over his shoulder and Nick took advantage of his weakness to redouble his efforts. Herman slipped backwards and then over the side, but as he fell he threw out a hand and grabbed Nick's arm, dragging him forward.

Both men dropped from view.

Montgomery shuffled along the seat hoping that Nick had saved himself and that he'd be clinging on to the side of the wagon, but both men were tumbling along the ground in a cloud of dust. Worse, the men they'd left behind were still making their way towards them, and the sight of Nick's plight had encouraged them to speed up.

Nick came to rest and shook himself then looked

up at the advancing men. He glanced at the wagon, then set off for it, but slowly and hobbling. Behind him Herman got to his feet. He moved unsteadily, as he set off after Nick with a shuffling gait.

Montgomery tore his gaze away from seeing how his young friend fared and concentrated on turning the wagon to go back for him. The horses were managing a good pace as they cantered along beside the outcrop, and they had now halved the distance to the place where, earlier, he'd found the bones. So it took Montgomery over a minute to slow them sufficiently to turn, take them downhill for a short distance, then make his way back towards the outcrop.

When Nick came back into view, he'd given up chasing after the wagon and was seeking cover on the outcrop. The following men had moved round to outflank him and they were edging him in to the rocks.

The outcrop was climbable, but if he tried it, Montgomery wouldn't be able to rescue him.

He hurried the wagon on, aiming to reach him while he was still on open ground, but Nick didn't look in his direction and continued to run towards the outcrop. Montgomery was fifty yards away when he disappeared behind a large boulder.

At his heels Herman followed him. Pike and Snyder were still struggling to catch up. Montgomery reckoned if he could reach the boulder before they did Nick might still be able to get on to the wagon. But when he could see the other side of the boulder he saw that Nick had actually headed into a recess.

Montgomery had no idea whether the recess would provide an escape route through the outcrop. But he figured that so far Nick had proved himself to be resourceful and so he backed his judgement by swerving the wagon away from the outcrop, then coming in straight on to it.

He was pleased that he had done this when, closer to, he saw that Nick was running away from Herman down a gully that appeared wide enough to accept the wagon and to present the possibility that it cut through the outcrop.

As Montgomery headed into the gully Nick slipped out of view to the left. At a slower pace than before Montgomery followed, gaining on Herman with every turn of the wheels.

Herman heard him coming and cast a worried glance over his shoulder. Then, on seeing the wagon bearing down on him, he flung himself to one side.

Montgomery trundled past him, then looked out for Herman trying to make a move to climb on to the wagon, but he just lay where he'd fallen. He watched the wagon head on by, only getting to his feet after Montgomery had passed.

Montgomery allowed himself a moment of hope that maybe he and Nick would be able to escape, then he concentrated on manoeuvring the wagon around the tight corner.

He was going too fast. The wagon swung round and one side crashed into the rocky wall. The wheels clattered over rough ground, causing Montgomery to rise from his seat, but he crashed back down, then clung on with one hand while fighting to steer a steady course with the other.

Then he looked up. He winced. The gully narrowed down to a thin exit that gave on to the plains beyond; it was too narrow for the wagon to pass through.

He glanced over his shoulder to see Herman trotting around the corner, his confident gait showing he knew that Montgomery had trapped himself.

Desperately Montgomery looked around, but the sides of the gully were too close for him to turn the wagon and they were probably too steep to climb. The only hope was to follow Nick on foot.

Montgomery slowed the wagon and while it was still moving he jumped down. Herman was thirty yards behind him and Pike and Snyder had just come around the corner, cutting off that escape route.

So he hurried after Nick, who had reached the narrow pass and now looked back to check that Montgomery was following. Montgomery shooed him on, so Nick carried on through the gap. He ran for thirty yards until he reached the exit. But then he skidded to a halt.

'Keep going,' Montgomery shouted, but Nick stood immobile.

As Montgomery came closer he saw that Nick was staring down at something on the ground beyond the pass. Montgomery continued to urge him to move on, but as the area beyond became visible he saw what had shocked Nick.

He slid to a halt beside him.

The body they'd found earlier today wasn't the only person to have suffered a gruesome fate recently. Another body lay staked out on the ground, its form a wind-dried husk.

Montgomery patted Nick on the back and urged him on.

'Come on,' he said. 'We can't help this one, but we can help ourselves.'

Nick gulped. Then, with an uncertain shrug, he moved off, speeding as the peril of their situation came back to him. They'd managed only a few paces skirting along beside the rocks to avoid the body when a man stepped out before them, a gun drawn and aimed at them.

'That's far enough, Montgomery,' he said.

Montgomery stomped to a halt. This man hadn't been amongst those who had brought them here. But he'd met him before. It had been a long time ago, but there was no mistaking him.

He was Lomax Rhinehart.

CHAPTER 9

Montgomery leaned forward preparing to run at Lomax Rhinehart and then wrest the gun from his grasp. But Lomax saw the movement and backed away for a pace while centring the gun on his chest.

Montgomery rocked back down on his heels and glanced over his shoulder to see Herman hurry out from the pass.

Herman cast only a brief glance at the body, proving he knew the remains were here and that they'd planned to bring their captives to this spot. Then he turned to face them with his arms held out ready to grab them if they ran towards him.

'So,' Montgomery said, 'I was right. You have joined Arnold Hays.'

'And I was right,' Lomax said. 'An idiot like you should never have been in charge of me.'

Montgomery smiled, giving the impression that he was acquiescing. Satisfied, Lomax flicked his gaze to Herman. Montgomery took that as his only chance and launched himself forward, hoping to catch Lomax unawares.

He'd managed two long paces before Lomax looked back at him, but then a whirling sound heralded a rope rasping down around his neck and pulling him up.

Montgomery glanced down to see a lasso wrapped around him. Pike and Snyder had arrived, having slipped out of the pass unheard.

Nick also set off, aiming to run to safety, but a second lasso twirled and with unerring accuracy Pike roped him. Nick struggled, trying to unwrap the rope from around his chest, while Montgomery stayed still. His rope had looped around his neck and his captor's gesture of a knife across the throat said that a sharp tug would throttle him.

Presently Nick admitted defeat. Now, surrounded, roped and with weapons held on them they had no choice but to accept their fate.

The next fifteen minutes were traumatic.

With Lomax holding a gun on them the other three men pushed them to the ground, then tied ropes to their wrists and ankles. Then they were splayed out and secured to stakes.

Montgomery looked for any opportunity to mount an escape attempt, figuring that being shot would be preferable to the terrible slow death that awaited. But the men worked with ruthless and practised efficiency, proving they had done this before.

When they stood back Montgomery strained, but

his bonds were tight. All he could do was offer Nick comfort.

He raised himself as much as he was able and tried to catch Nick's eye, but Nick had withdrawn into himself and was staring upwards while murmuring to himself, perhaps in prayer.

Lomax interrupted his efforts by letting his shadow fall over Montgomery's face. When Montgomery looked up, Lomax's form was a dark outline with the sun creating a halo effect around his head, which was in sharp contrast to the cruel knife he held aloft.

'I should thank you for returning my knife,' he said.

'Releasing Nick will show you mean that.'

'Your concern for this one is touching.' Lomax pointed at Nick. 'So I'll work on him first and let you enjoy hearing his screams for the help you can never provide.'

Montgomery jerked his head in the opposite direction to signify the dried-out husk lying beside him.

'Was your previous victim someone who also wanted my help?'

Lomax smiled and turned away from Nick to consider the body.

'You'll get precious little comfort in your final hours, but I'll put your mind at rest on that. Wallace Sheckley is lying beside you, and at the last he did hope you'd save him, but then again he babbled about many things.'

Lomax moved purposfully towards Nick and, in desperation, hoping to keep him talking and so buy Nick a few more moments, Montgomery blurted out a retort.

'What did he say?'

'You can't stop me. Nothing anyone has ever said has stopped me.' Lomax stood over Nick. He appraised his form with an eager gleam in his eye, his knife twitching as he debated where to start.

'But you're too decent a man to do this,' Montgomery snapped, desperation making him say the opposite to what he thought. 'Twenty years ago we were fighting on the same side against the men you did this to. You don't need to side with Arnold Hays.'

Lomax gathered up a stone.

'Wallace tried that approach too, but I told him the truth before the end.' He laughed as he whetted the already sharp blade. 'I am not the kind of man who would side with Arnold Hays.'

'Then why do this?'

For long moments Lomax didn't reply as he looked at Nick then at the knife. But, perhaps because Nick was avoiding his eye and so was providing no entertainment, he turned to Montgomery.

'Because I don't work for Arnold Hays. I'm helping the townsfolk.'

Pike and Snyder muttered supportive grunts while Herman moved into Montgomery's eyeline. He gave

Lomax a firm glare, and Lomax returned a worried glance that suggested that even if he had just told the truth there was tension between them.

'But you're about to kill us. You're doing Arnold Hays's dirty work.'

'I'm not killing you. I'm saving my friends' lives.' Lomax waved his free hand, his eyes alighting with passion for the first time. 'I don't live in the fort. I live in Sunrise. They are my people, and so I'll do whatever I have to do to help them, just like I did back in the days when we were on the same side.'

'I don't understand,' Montgomery murmured.

Even to his own ears his tone had sounded resigned and different from his previous obvious attempts to delay the inevitable. Lomax must have picked up on this as he fixed Montgomery with a cold gaze that bored into him.

'When we rebelled against Arnold Hays he killed ten men. We killed only one of his men and so he taunted us that they were worth ten of us. Last month we tried again. We ambushed one of his men outside the saloon then moved on to get the others, but it went wrong. The rest lost heart and the rebellion died before it'd got started.'

'I can believe that,' Montgomery said with a rueful glance at his bonds.

'Arnold decreed a terrible revenge. We'd killed one of his men, so he'd kill another ten townsfolk. The attack happened outside James's saloon, so James had to pick who those ten would be. Wallace had come looking for me, so he picked him first, but that still left nine people to die.'

Lomax frowned, as if the tale really did trouble him. There was only one body here, so Montgomery prompted him.

'What did he do?'

'I stepped in and saved nine lives. Wallace didn't thank me none.' Lomax brandished the knife, reflecting the sun into Montgomery's eyes and forcing him to look away. 'I promised Arnold I'd make him suffer for ten. And I did.'

Montgomery could think of nothing to say to this and in the silence Herman spoke up.

'Arnold promised you it'd be two this time and three the next. But he knows you've resorted to kid-napping passers-by to use as fodder when your pathetic attempts to take him on fail. So the next time the ones who will die will all be townsfolk.' Herman gave Lomax a long glare. 'And they'll be people who are of no use to him.'

Lomax nodded, getting the hint of what he needed to do to keep himself off that list. He knelt beside Nick's chest.

Nick jerked his head to look the other way, so Lomax grabbed his chin and drew him back to look at him. Slowly he moved the knife into Nick's eyeline.

Montgomery turned away, unable to watch what happened next and unable to think of anything he could say or do that would stop it.

He had misunderstood the situation and he was

caught between the ruthless Arnold who wanted blood and the heartless Lomax who would give it to him.

He couldn't side with either party, but with Lomax about to begin his terrible work there was only one person who could help him. He caught Herman's eye.

'Stop him,' he said.

'No,' Herman said, then grinned with a twinkle in his eye that said he remembered what Montgomery and Nick had done to him back in Sunrise. 'Wallace pleaded until Lomax silenced him. I know your story, so save your breath. You fought together. You fell out. You've sought Lomax out to kill him.'

From the corner of his eye Montgomery saw Lomax stiffen and rock back on to his haunches to watch him.

Clearly the mention of their shared past had concerned him, and Montgomery reckoned he knew why. He had nothing with which to bargain for his life, except for one long shot.

As this would be his only chance, he took a while to reply and ensured his voice sounded more assured than he felt.

'You don't know the real reason I sought out Lomax, but perhaps you should.'

Herman shrugged, looking as if he wouldn't respond, but then curiosity got the better of him and he stood over Montgomery.

'What is it?'

Montgomery jerked his head back signifying that Herman should lean in closer.

'I'm not after him for revenge. I'm after him for the gold.'

Lomax didn't move, but his lack of a reaction appeared so suspicious that Herman raised an eyebrow.

'I'd not heard that before. How much?'

'Twenty bars.' Montgomery waited until Herman licked his lips with anticipation. 'We stole it, but Lomax double-crossed us.'

Herman glanced at Lomax. 'Is this right?'

'Of course it isn't,' Lomax spluttered. 'He's just trying to bargain for his life. You heard Wallace's pleas. You know they'll say anything when they're about to die.'

'I do, but Wallace didn't offer anything as interesting as twenty gold bars.'

'He didn't, so if it were true, he would have.'

Herman conceded this was a good point with a firm nod. Then he folded his arms in a slow manner that said Montgomery had one final chance to persuade him. After that, he wouldn't listen.

Montgomery took a deep breath. 'Of course Wallace wouldn't mention it. He was the one who was trying to catch us.'

'He wasn't,' Lomax snapped. 'Wallace tried to stop me getting the gold from—'

Herman darted his head to the side to consider Lomax, who gave a sharp intake of breath as he realized the mistake he'd just made.

'That,' Herman said, 'is some very interesting information.'

'Montgomery came after me,' Lomax murmured, not meeting his eye. 'But there was never any gold.'

'There'd better be or you'll take Montgomery's place.' Herman gestured to Pike. 'Untie them and I'll take them to the fort. Arnold Hays can find out the truth.'

CHAPTER 10

Herman pushed Montgomery to his knees in front of Arnold Hays.

Montgomery landed heavily and toppled over on to his side where he lay recovering his breath, not that he minded the rough treatment. Thirty minutes ago he had been expecting to die a slow and painful death.

Now he at least had hope, even if it was a small one.

Herman and the townsfolk had taken him along with Nick and Lomax to the fort. Although outnumbered Herman had controlled Pike and Snyder with ease and they'd not tried to help Lomax. Whether that was because they distrusted him as much as Montgomery did, or because they were downtrodden, he didn't know.

Arnold Hays was sitting outside, sheltering from the lowering sun under the porch of what had been the officers' quarters. Lined up on either side were the men who had joined him in town earlier.

He listened with undisguised scepticism to Herman's explanation of why he and Nick had been saved. The mention of gold gathered only a snort of derision, which encouraged several men to pour scorn on the prospect of the offer being genuine.

When Herman had finished he lowered his head and nervously shuffled from foot to foot, clearly expecting retribution for his actions rather than praise.

'You were right to bring them to me,' Arnold said after a long consideration, this comment dragging a relieved sigh from Herman's lips. 'But I don't believe the story.'

Lomax smirked at Montgomery then took a pace forward.

'In that case let me finish what I started,' he said. 'I'll make Montgomery's screams—'

'Get back,' Arnold muttered. 'I indulge your tastes when they help me, but that doesn't give you the right to tell me what to do. And I will get to the truth.'

Arnold gestured and three men stepped forward. They each grabbed one of their new captives and manoeuvred them towards the nearest building.

Montgomery didn't struggle, figuring that he'd expected to die so he'd accept imprisonment. Nick also went quietly, but Lomax fought his attacker and threw him off, forcing another man to step up and help the first drag him along.

Lomax shouted and fought for every step of the way, but they still led him to the door. The building was a large square construction which, when one man dragged open the door, turned out to have walls that were a yard thick, suggesting it had probably been an armoury.

Lomax continued to struggle, so his captors moved to shove him through the door first, but when they were in the doorway Arnold called out for them to halt.

'You ready to listen?' Lomax said, the demand making Arnold snort with anger.

'Two will still die,' he said, pointing at Lomax. 'When I open up the armoury I will either have the truth about the gold or I will pick the ringleaders of your latest rebellion.'

Arnold gestured and the men pushed Lomax inside, where he went sprawling on his knees. Then they shoved Montgomery and Nick in after him and slammed the thick door shut behind them.

A heavy latch fell into place as the light level cut off to just a thin stream outlining the door. Lomax lay in that line of light, staring at the floor and breathing deeply.

'You know what that taunt means, don't you?' he said, his tone hollow and haunted.

'I understand,' Montgomery said. 'Arnold wants blood and he'll choose two people from amongst the townsfolk to provide it.'

Montgomery knew that that threat should

99

concern him but, since they had surrendered then callously turned their backs on him, right now he couldn't bring himself to care.

'I know, and those ringleaders will be two from Dean, James and . . . and Elizabeth.'

'If you really do live in Sunrise, then that might worry you, so maybe you should save them and tell Arnold about the gold.'

'The truth about the gold is what Arnold put us in here to decide.' Lomax slowly moved round until he was sitting facing them. He grinned. 'The door is locked. None of us is going anywhere. And so we can decide the matter between us.'

Montgomery nodded. For twenty years he had hoped he would one day get the chance to make Lomax pay for his crimes, and now it would seem that fate had provided him with that chance.

He nudged Nick, urging him to retreat into a corner. Then he moved along the wall into the shadows. Nick glanced at Montgomery, then at Lomax, but with some reluctance he did as ordered.

'Are you going to tell me about the gold first?' Montgomery said, flexing his fists. 'So I can save my own life afterwards.'

Lomax snorted with grim humour. 'You won't get the chance. I'll be the one who explains the situation to Arnold, and you two's deaths should satisfy him.'

Montgomery shook his head, words of anger on his lips, but they died when, with relish, Lomax reached to his boot and withdrew a short knife. The blade caught a stray beam of light, highlighting its sharp edge.

Lomax got to his feet and crouched with the knife thrust out. Then, with an eager gleam in his eye, he backed away to the wall behind him. He reached back and slapped it. Then he walked to the wall to his left and slapped that.

His gestures made it obvious that they were trapped in this room and there was no way to avoid this fight.

'Stay in the corner,' Montgomery said to Nick.

Nick shook his head and moved over to stand beside Montgomery.

'If he's got a knife,' he said, 'I'm not keeping back. We can get him together.'

Lomax chuckled with confidence. 'A man with a knife is worth two men without one.'

'But not,' Nick said, 'when the man with the knife is as worthless as you are.'

This taunt made Lomax shift his attention away from Montgomery and move in towards Nick. Montgomery reckoned that that had been Nick's plan. If he could make Lomax divide his attention between them, that would give them their best chance of avoiding the blade.

The room was twenty feet square. Montgomery's eyes now having become accustomed to the low light level, he could see that there were no obstacles or even dirt on the floor that he could kick into Lomax's face.

So he moved to the side, as did Nick. Lomax followed their motion and slowly the three men closed on each other while circling.

They'd completed a full circle when Lomax made his first aggressive move. He darted in and swung a wild scything blow at Nick's chest, who danced to the side easily letting the blade whistle by several feet short.

Lomax laughed. 'You sure are scared of this blade. I can't wait to see you bleed.'

Nick gave a quick beckoning gesture. 'And I can't wait to see you get your own knife stuck in your throat.'

Lomax moved in again, but this time Nick was moving past a corner. He had to press his back to the wall to evade the blade, then scurry off to the next corner to avoid reprisals. Lomax uttered a confident snort of laughter as he watched Nick's ungainly progress.

Then he followed him, seeking to trap him in the next corner, but Nick scampered away. So Lomax stomped to a halt, then moved in the opposite direction, aiming to catch him when he came round to meet him.

Montgomery reckoned Nick had done enough for now in taking Lomax on. He spread his arms to get Lomax's attention. Then he took slow paces towards him. Lomax stopped and shifted his attention back to him.

Montgomery halted just out of the range of

Lomax's knife arm, then rocked from side looking for an opening where he could reach him without being stabbed. He feinted to Lomax's left, but Lomax didn't move and instead he favoured him with a grin that said he knew what Montgomery would do next.

Despite his apparent confident air, Montgomery again feinted, and again he was ignored. He feinted to his right, then, in rapid change of direction he went to his left. And this time he followed through.

He had aimed to leap forward and barge into Lomax's legs with his body and topple him, but Lomax followed his movement and thrust his right hand down.

The knife arced towards Montgomery. It would have sliced into his shoulder if he hadn't stopped his motion and converted it into a roll to the side and away from Lomax.

Lomax jerked forward to follow him, but then Nick used the opening to attempt what Montgomery had tried. He threw himself forward.

Again the quick-witted Lomax turned on his heel and scythed the knife around, forcing Nick to slide to a halt then dance backwards with his arms spread. The knife whistled through the air a few inches short of his exposed chest.

Montgomery was still lying where he'd landed. Lomax followed through with a second wild slash. This time Nick stood his ground and ducked away from the blow.

The blade sliced through a trailing sleeve, narrowly missing flesh, but now, with them being so close together, Nick risked lunging for Lomax's knife arm.

His fingers brushed Lomax's forearm, but in his first desperate act Lomax tore his arm away then thrust a short-armed jab at Nick's belly. Only Nick's hunched stance saved him and the blade merely sliced through his jacket to emerge short of his held-in stomach.

Montgomery was now rolling to his feet, but Nick didn't wait for him to provide a distraction. He scrambled out of range. He managed a single pace but in his haste his ankle turned and he stumbled to his knees.

With a cry of triumph Lomax darted forward aiming to stick Nick in the kidneys from behind. But the apparent opportunity took his attention away from Montgomery and Montgomery made him pay.

He charged at him, giving himself no chance of moving away if Lomax turned on him. He pounded for three long paces then leapt forward as Lomax lunged with what would have been a crippling blow.

With his feet off the floor Montgomery slammed into Lomax's side and knocked him over before the knife could cut into the downed man. The two men hit the floor and then rolled over, their limbs entangled.

When they came to a halt Montgomery was lying on top of Lomax, but he didn't have a grip of

Lomax's knife hand, so he raised himself while reaching for it. From the corner of his eye he saw light flash as Lomax tore his arm up from the ground. The knife came round, aiming for his neck.

Montgomery flinched away, then continued the motion and rolled. He expected to feel the blade stab into him from behind, but he rolled once, then twice without pain. Then he fetched up against the wall.

His head jarred against the stone. Momentarily stunned, he took valuable seconds to gather his senses. But when he moved to rise he was too late. Lomax had followed him and was already putting all his strength into a slashing blow that would rip into his face.

Montgomery threw up an arm to take the blow while wincing. Instinctively he closed his eyes in expectation of being sliced, but the knife didn't connect and when he opened them, to his surprise he saw that Nick had neutralized the threat of the knife.

There was nothing in the room that they could use to take on Lomax, so Nick had improvised by removing his jacket and using it as a makeshift restraint. Now his jacket was wrapped around Lomax's knife hand and Lomax was struggling to wrest it free.

Montgomery got to his feet as Lomax flexed his arm. Then, with a twist of his wrist, he wrenched his hand loose, but the movement was too brisk and he lost his grip of the knife. A streak of light marked the knife's passage as it hurtled to the roof.

Montgomery didn't need to wait for a second opportunity and with his head down he charged Lomax. He caught him full in the chest with a leading shoulder, then drove him onwards across the room.

Lomax back-stepped for several paces, then Montgomery's relentless motion proved to be too strong for him and he went down heavily, to land sprawling on his back. Montgomery landed on top of him.

With Lomax's advantage gone Montgomery bunched a fist and hammered it downwards with a pulverizing blow to the face that crashed the back of Lomax's head against the floor.

'Had enough?' Montgomery demanded, settling himself on Lomax's stomach with his fist drawn back.

All Lomax could provide for an answer was a bleated murmur. Montgomery glanced up to check that Nick had found the knife, then moved his knees up to press them down on Lomax's shoulders and pin him to the floor.

He gave Lomax enough time to gather his senses then drew his attention to the knife in Nick's hand.

'Get it over with,' Lomax murmured, 'if you've got the guts.'

'I've got the guts and I'm prepared to find out what colour your guts are, but that's not what I want.'

'You won't get no answers out of me about the gold.'

Montgomery sighed. Then, with a contemptuous swipe, he thudded his fist into Lomax's face. This time Lomax slumped.

Montgomery waited with his fist held back for him to stir, but when Lomax didn't move, he slapped his face. His head lolled. He was out cold, and that was fine with Montgomery. It gave him time to think.

Slowly, in case his apparent unconscious state was a trap, he rolled off him, then dragged him over to the wall where he propped him up. Then he joined Nick, meaning to congratulate him, but Nick was looking upwards.

'We both need to keep an eye on him,' Montgomery said, 'while we work out how we can make him talk about the gold.'

Nick shook his head then pointed out what had interested him on the roof.

'We don't need no answers from him,' he said, 'to get out of here.'

Montgomery looked up, then narrowed his eyes when he saw what had interested Nick.

When Nick had torn the knife free it had clattered into the roof, Montgomery could now see that the roof was wooden. A chink of light was shining down like a small star where the knife had bored a hole in it.

'You could be right,' Montgomery said, slapping him on the shoulder, 'provided we can get up there before he comes round.'

CHAPTER 11

Montgomery slid down the wall to the floor then rocked backwards to land on his rump, as he'd done on his last five attempts.

The wall had been well built and the cracks between the stone blocks were just wide enough for him to cram his fingertips inside. But that didn't give him enough leverage to support his weight and he'd yet managed to get even halfway to the roof.

Now the light level was dropping, making it harder for him to see whether any section of the wall had crumbled enough to provide purchase. Forlornly he peered up at the chink of light that had given them hope of escape. It was only a few yards away, but it felt further.

'Let me try,' Nick said.

'You're watching Lomax,' Montgomery said. 'I'll deal with the escape.'

'Except you'll never get us out, and I've had an idea.' Nick waved the knife he'd taken off Lomax.

'We need something to help with the climbing, and this is all we have.'

Montgomery considered the short blade, then shook his head.

'That'll never support my weight.'

'It won't.' Nick smiled, letting Montgomery know he was resisting the urge to offer an insult. 'So I'll use it while you watch Lomax.'

Montgomery spread his hands. 'You've got as much right as I have to break your neck.'

Nick nodded then moved over to the wall leaving Montgomery to check on Lomax. He confirmed that he hadn't moved since he'd slumped after banging his head.

Then, kneeling in the centre of the room, Montgomery kept one eye on him and the other on Nick as he made better progress than he'd managed.

Nick worked carefully, seeking to ensure he had to climb only once. He scraped out the dirt and mortar from between the stone blocks until he'd created a gap. Then he lifted himself up.

When he'd steadied himself he gripped the wall with one hand while scraping with the other at the furthest extent of his reach until he had a big enough gap to take his weight again.

Montgomery had to admit Nick had had both a good idea and was progressing with greater agility than he had managed. Within the time it would have taken Montgomery to fall off three times Nick reached the top of the wall and stood beneath the section of roof where the gap had formed. He tucked the knife in his belt then tapped the roof, probing around in an expanding circle.

'The wood's rotten,' he whispered. 'But only in a small area.'

He scraped the roof with his fingers, producing a cascade of papery wood fragments, showing that either water had collected here and seeped into the grain or gnawing animals had done their work.

'Work quietly,' Montgomery whispered. 'I don't think any guards are outside, but don't risk it.'

'I might not have a choice,' Nick said, breaking off to hug the wall. 'This isn't easy.'

Montgomery resisted the urge to provide more suggestions and let Nick concentrate on his work.

For the next ten minutes Nick probed with either his fingers or with the knife, gradually widening the hole. Then, with a sudden crack of timber, a two-foot length of wood came away.

Nick jerked away from it to grab hold of the wall while Montgomery ducked to avoid the falling wood. When he was sure no more pieces would follow it down, he picked up the broken plank, finding that it was solid for most of its length.

Then he looked up to see that Nick had created a gap that was about a foot wide and two feet long. He was also shaking as the strain of holding himself up became too demanding.

'Come down and try again later,' Montgomery urged.

'I don't reckon that'll help,' Nick whispered. He poked the wood on either side of the gap. 'That's all that's going to come down easily. The rest of the wood is solid. Even if I work on it all night I'll never break through with this small knife.'

'That hole's too small to get through.'

Nick looked down and sighed. 'For you it is.'

Montgomery made a shooing away gesture.

'Then if you can get out, do it. Just keep going and—'

'I'm not abandoning you.'

Montgomery set his hands on his hips meaning to argue, but he had heard the determination in Nick's voice.

'Then do whatever you can while you're out there, but if you can't help, I understand.'

'I will return and I will get you out.' Nick moved to throw the knife down, but Montgomery shook his head.

'You need it more than I do.' Montgomery brandished the wood. 'I can defend myself with this.'

For long moments Nick looked down at Montgomery, appearing from the hunched set of his shoulders that he wanted to continue discussing the matter. Then, with a murmured comment to himself, he looked up and started to work out how he would get through the hole.

Experimentally he slipped an arm through the gap and he must have found something to grab hold of as he drew himself up then scraped his feet against the stone as he sought purchase.

With more noise than Montgomery would have liked him to make, he prised himself through the hole until only his feet were dangling. Then he disappeared from view.

A few moments later his face appeared peering down at Montgomery through the hole. He offered a beaming smile and Montgomery returned a supportive nod. Then he moved away.

Feet pattered over the roof, then scraping sounded as he sought a way down. Then there was silence.

Montgomery welcomed the quiet and for the next few minutes he continued to hope for silence as this meant Nick hadn't been discovered.

How Nick would get him out he didn't know, but at least he now had a chance. When, after some moments, he accepted that Nick hadn't been discovered immediately, he concentrated on watching Lomax.

Several minutes later he heard a groan. Then Lomax stirred and looked around.

'So you didn't kill me,' he murmured, fingering his bruised cheek.

'Not yet,' Montgomery said.

Nick stomped to a halt to empty the sand from his boots then resumed his steady trudge towards town.

The sun had risen three hours ago and that had at least made his journey feel more cheering, but he hadn't enjoyed his long walk.

Last night he had searched the fort carefully, but two men had been patrolling beside the main gate and they were close enough to the armoury to see him if he went in any direction other than away from them.

He had then searched the unoccupied buildings for something he could use to get Montgomery out of the armoury, but they had been empty. By the time the guards had been changed he'd decided he wouldn't be able to find anything useful. Sunrise was his only option.

He'd walked through most of the night, stopping for a few hours of intermittent sleep in the dead of night before resuming his journey. Now he was approaching the town and so far he'd seen no signs of life ahead.

On the edge of town he veered away from the main drag and made his way around the backs of the buildings to reach the stables. A quick search inside revealed several horses and, even better, he found a length of rope and a hammer.

As he also wanted to return with a weapon that was more substantial than the knife, he was putting his mind to how he might obtain a gun when a voice piped up behind him.

'What you doing in here?'

Nick swirled round to find he was facing Dean, the one man he had hoped he might meet when he returned.

'I've come back for you,' he said, setting his hands on his hips.

Dean paled, looking as if he'd seen a ghost, which he might well have done based on what he must think had happened to Nick. It took Dean several seconds to find his voice and then he could manage only a bleat. He shuffled inside the building and approached Nick cautiously.

'Is that you, Nick?' he asked, narrowing his eyes.

'It sure is.' Nick folded his arms. 'Why are you so shocked? You didn't expect that something bad would happen to me, did you?'

'I'm . . .' Dean spread his hands. 'I'm pleased to see you . . . escaped.'

His comment sounded honest, but Nick still sneered.

'And why would a double-crosser like you be pleased?'

'Because I didn't want to turn on you, but I had no choice. We weren't going to win that battle.'

Nick sneered. 'The townsfolk were making headway. Montgomery had captured Arnold Hays and we'd pinned his men down. If everyone had done what they were supposed to do, we'd have prevailed.'

'Perhaps.' Dean kicked at the ground. 'But we couldn't risk it. They must have told you Arnold's rule. If we'd killed any of them, he'd have made us all pay.'

Nick nodded. 'So your options were to see it

114

through and wipe out all his men, or back out quickly?'

'That's what we agreed. We thought you and Montgomery might win through, but you weren't doing that and. . . .' Dean's voice faded to a croak and he lowered his head, perhaps accepting how bad his excuses had sounded.

'You'll only prevail if you all stand together, but not one of you has the guts to do that, so one day soon this town will die. And that's what you deserve.'

'You're right,' Dean murmured. 'I'm sorry for what we did.'

'You will be. Montgomery escaped too, and the last we heard Arnold was still determined to seek retribution, only from another two people.'

Dean looked up and gulped. 'Then we need help.'

'You do, but you're not getting it from me.' Nick walked up to Dean and held out a hand. 'I need a gun. Give me yours and I won't make your problems any worse.'

Dean opened his mouth to retort, then with a sigh he closed it. He unlooped his gunbelt and held it out.

'I hope you get away,' he said, then stood aside.

If Dean had said or done anything other than offer complete contrition Nick would have led a horse from the stables and then ridden back to the fort, but his ashamed-sounding tone couldn't let him do that. He contemplated Dean.

'I don't have to go,' he said.

Hope lit Dean's eyes. 'You mean you'll help us?'

'Maybe, but only if you'll help me. I didn't tell you the whole story. Montgomery is still a prisoner back at the fort. I intend to rescue him and if you're to avoid reprisals, this time you have to face up to Arnold Hays.'

Dean nodded and stood tall, seemingly pleased that the matter would come to a head.

'We need to talk James round and then he'll work on the rest before Pike and Snyder can sow doubt.'

Nick nodded. Then he gestured ahead for Dean to lead on to the saloon.

On the way they said nothing more and, as he expected, when he walked into the saloon, he received everyone's undivided attention. Like Dean, the few customers stared at him with open-mouthed surprise.

'I might well be dead,' Nick said with his hands on his hips as he cast his gaze around the saloon, 'after all the help you provided.'

His comment generated a long silence. At last a customer sitting at one of the tables spoke up.

'So Arnold let you go, did he?'

Nick turned. At first he couldn't see who had spoken, but then several men moved backwards and let him see that Pike and Snyder were sitting watching him.

Nick had thought they'd stayed at the fort, and from the surprised looks everyone was giving him, clearly they hadn't reported on the events there. This

116

gave further credence to Dean's explanation that these two men were the main obstacles he faced in persuading everyone to take on Arnold.

'He doesn't know I've gone,' Nick said, 'but when he finds out, you know what he'll want. For some reason you haven't told anyone about it.'

Pike narrowed his eyes. Then he glanced at Snyder, who, with a co-ordinated movement, joined him in rising. Both men's hands strayed towards their holsters.

'And we'll be dealing with that matter,' Snyder said, 'just as soon as we've disposed of you.'

CHAPTER 12

'So is your young friend coming back?' Lomax asked. This was the first thing he'd said since last night's fight.

'He will,' Montgomery said. 'What we do then is up to you.'

Lomax frowned, acknowledging the trickiness of their situation.

Since Nick had escaped last night the two men had sat facing each other on opposite sides of the armoury.

The almost complete darkness meant that Lomax could have approached him undetected, and so for many hours Montgomery had clutched his only weapon, the length of wood Nick had knocked from the roof. But Lomax hadn't attacked him and after a while Montgomery had relaxed enough to fall into a fitful sleep.

Daylight had brought confirmation that Lomax hadn't moved.

Since then his occasional fingering of his bruised

head had been his only movement. They had both drawn in their breath several times when they'd heard movement outside, but the door had remained closed.

'I don't reckon,' Lomax said, 'he'll get back before his escape is discovered, so everyone is doomed – you, me, the townsfolk.'

Montgomery acknowledged this was his own main concern with a nod. If the guards discovered only two men were inside the armoury it was unlikely anything they could say would save them.

'I guess so. If we escape, more of the townsfolk will die, and despite everything they did I wouldn't wish that on them. But if we don't, then there's still the matter of our differences to sort out.' Montgomery raised his plank. 'Perhaps we should sort them out now.'

Lomax eyed the wood without interest.

'I can't tell you about the gold.' Lomax's jutting jaw conveyed that he was thinking about whether he should continue. Then, with a resigned frown, he spoke. 'Because there never was any.'

'I don't believe that.' Montgomery thought back, searching his memory for the facts. 'I know people who saw the shipment.'

'It sure did exist.' Lomax frowned. 'I mean it never went missing in the way we thought it had. Those wretches raided the convoy, but you saw them. They were so weak they barely had the strength to stand up, never mind take on thirty heavily armed men.'

Montgomery narrowed his eyes. 'But the gold did go missing.'

'It did, but they didn't take it. Sometimes the people on your side are worse than the enemy.' Lomax paused while Montgomery gave a rueful snort. 'Some officers probably stole it and then blamed it on the raiders.'

'Is that what they claimed before you took them apart?'

'They said plenty.' Lomax shrugged. 'Not that I believe anything anyone says in that situation.'

'You've had more experience of that than I've had, so I can't argue with you.'

Lomax pointed a firm finger at him. 'Don't start whining about the plight of those poor renegades. We saw what they did to their victims. I showed them the same mercy.'

'And twenty years later you're still doing it.'

'You've got me wrong.' Lomax glanced around their darkened prison and when he spoke his tone was wistful. 'After I fled your company I roamed around, first to escape the men who were after me, and then to try to find somewhere to fit in.'

'I can imagine that would have been hard for you.'

Lomax glared at him for a few moments before he continued.

'It took many years, but eventually I fetched up in Sunrise. I decided it was a good place and I settled down. I found me a good woman and for a while life was good.'

Montgomery raised his eyebrows. 'That doesn't sound like you.'

Lomax licked his lips, clearly relishing his next comment.

'Do you find it that hard to believe that a woman like Elizabeth would like a man like me?'

Montgomery couldn't stop his mouth falling open, providing his answer.

'I assume she doesn't know about your appetites?'

'I have no appetites. I do what is necessary to survive. I had my revenge on those men twenty years ago, but I've done nothing like that since. Then one day Arnold Hays rode into town and he tried to take it all away. Since then I've done what I had to do.'

'And I might have believed you if I hadn't have seen how much you were enjoying yourself when you had me and Nick pinned out.'

'You see what you want to see.'

'I do, and that means I'll make my own judgement on your punishment.' Montgomery glanced at the door. 'But that won't matter none if Arnold just drags us out of here and kills us, so have you got any ideas on how we can stop that happening?'

'Are you saying we should work together like we used to do twenty years ago?'

Montgomery snorted. 'I didn't say that. But we do need to work out what we'll do, or we'll die.'

Lomax shrugged. 'Then we die.'

*

'At least you two are being open now,' Nick said, eyeing the gun-toting Pike and Snyder.

The two men edged apart. Snyder stayed before the table at which they'd been sitting while Pike moved over to stand beside the bar.

'Everyone knows what we do,' Pike said. 'We keep this town safe.'

'You do, and at the same time you're taking away its only chance of living.' Nick risked looking away from them to run his gaze across the customers, searching their eyes for signs of support. He saw none, so he ended his perusal with the most likely candidates, James and Dean. 'Do you accept what they're doing here?'

James furrowed his brow making Dean try to catch his eye while the rest of the customers gave each other shamefaced looks.

'They leave us to deal with things,' Pike said settling his stance and drawing Nick's attention back to him.

The steeliness of that comment helped Nick to work out what was happening here. The townsfolk had turned a blind eye to what these men and Lomax Rhinehart were doing, but they didn't know all the details. They presumed that the people they'd picked had been taken away to be executed, but not that they had died in such a horrendous manner.

So the moment he tried to reveal this secret the two men would go for their guns. Nick was confident he could prevail against one of them, but not both.

'Then perhaps,' he said as his heart thudded and nervous sweat broke out on his forehead, 'nobody need know the truth.'

Pike narrowed his eyes, clearly expecting deception. He glanced at Snyder, but before he received an answer Dean stepped forward.

'What truth?' he asked.

This hint that the situation might turn for the worse panicked Snyder into scrambling for his gun. With Pike being half-turned away from him Nick turned on Snyder first.

He threw his hand to his holster, his gun coming to hand in a moment. Crouching he aimed and fired catching Snyder with a shot to the belly that sent him staggering backwards into a table.

He didn't wait to check whether he'd overcome him and turned to Pike. He didn't reckon he'd be able to dispose of Pike too. Sure enough, when he swung back Pike had already turned his gun on him.

A gunshot tore out, but to Nick's relief Pike staggered an uncertain pace to the side, his gun falling from his hand, the fingers of his left hand rising to touch the spreading bloom on his chest. Then he keeled over.

Nick looked to the bar to see that James had drawn a rifle up from under the bar and had shot him.

Then in short order Nick stepped past the prone Pike to check on Snyder. He found that he too was breathing his last.

Nick gulped, the feeling overcoming him that this was the first time he'd shot another man. He'd had no choice, but that didn't make him feel any better about the situation.

He didn't get time to dwell on the matter; Dean bade him to join him at the bar where he poured him a large whiskey. When Nick downed it, Dean gave him an encouraging pat on the back.

Nick murmured that he would be fine, and when James returned from dragging Pike and Snyder into a back room, he too offered his support with a wide smile.

'Obliged,' Nick said. 'You took what I was saying in good faith, and you did the right thing.'

'Before you say things like that,' James said, 'you need to know the full truth. Most people here didn't know what they were doing, but some of us did.'

'You?' Nick received a nod, then he looked at Dean, who gave a curt nod while gnawing at his bottom lip.

'I went out to the outcrop,' James said. 'I saw what they'd done to Wallace and told Dean. That persuaded us to fight back.'

'But not to see it through?'

James winced then lowered his head. 'We don't feel good about any of this.'

Nick sighed. 'The important thing is that you've now made the right choice.'

James gave an uncertain nod, which suggested that although he had helped him he still hadn't committed himself. Nick turned to Dean to see how he felt about the situation, but then to his surprise Dean grabbed his shoulders and shoved him along the bar.

Then he clamped a hand over his mouth, bent him double, and bundled him to the floor.

Nick struggled, while still being amazed that Dean had turned on him. But he couldn't free himself from Dean's firm hold and when he'd stopped pushing him he found he was lying behind the bar.

Dean bent down to whisper in his ear.

'Be quiet,' he urged.

Nick gave his answer when he tried to buck Dean away, but Dean bore down on him and held him immobile. Nick gathered his strength aiming to put all he had behind his next attempt. Then he heard heavy footfalls coming into the saloon and a new voice spoke up.

'I've been coming here too often these days for my liking.'

'Then do us all a favour,' James said, 'and stay away.'

An aggrieved grunt sounded. Then footfalls approached the bar. Nick was just placing where he'd heard the voice before when Dean whispered the answer to him.

'It's Herman.'

Nick gave up struggling, now accepting that Dean had helped him.

'I can't,' Herman said, 'when I have people to collect.'

'We decide who Arnold takes.'

'You did, but you've wriggled your way out of a difficult situation twice now, and so this time I'm choosing.' Herman gave a hollow laugh. 'And I'm taking Dean and Elizabeth.'

Dean tensed. Then, with a pat on the shoulder that urged Nick to stay down, he released his hold and stood. His appearance made Herman shuffle his feet as he moved round to face him.

'I'm not going with you,' Dean announced, 'and neither is Elizabeth or anyone else.'

'You will,' Herman said with quiet menace. 'Your only other option is to fight Arnold, and you people haven't got the guts to do that.'

CHAPTER 13

Montgomery judged that it was around noon when the armoury door rattled and murmuring sounded, heralding their release. There had been more than enough time for Nick to return and help them, even if he'd had to go back to Sunrise.

So it was likely he'd taken up Montgomery's offer and made good his escape. Whatever had happened, he wished him well.

After their brief conversation earlier he and Lomax hadn't spoken again and as the door swung open flooding the inside with light he glared at Montgomery.

'Anyone still alive in there?' one guard asked with laughter in his tone, giving Montgomery further hope that Nick hadn't been recaptured.

The guard stayed outside while holding a hand to his brow as he peered into the darker interior, which made Montgomery realize that he wouldn't be able to see inside easily.

'Most of us are,' Montgomery said standing and holding his hands up. 'But not the young one.'

Then, trying to preserve his subterfuge, he headed outside. Lomax must have caught on to what Montgomery was trying to do as he hurried on and slipped outside.

'But we still don't have an answer for Arnold,' he said.

The guard looked inside, suspicion narrowing his eyes, but then with a shrug he slammed the door shut and barred it.

'The young one can rot in there, then,' he said, 'and unless Arnold gets some answers, you'll both join him.'

They were led across the quadrangle to stand before Arnold, who was sitting in the same place as he had been in yesterday: under a porch outside the officers' quarters in the shade.

He was eating with his men, which he continued to do with relish while not acknowledging they'd arrived, adding to their discomfiture. Then the men passed around a full water-skin.

Montgomery and Lomax hadn't been fed or watered in the best part of a day. So now that he was out of the relative cool of the armoury, the sun was beating down on Montgomery's head and reminding him of his hunger and thirst.

As they drank, the men spilled most of the water on the ground, then grinned when they saw their captives lick their lips. Several minutes passed before

Arnold turned to them.

While gnawing on a bone he appraised them. When he'd stripped the meat he tossed the bone over a shoulder, wiped his greasy hands on his vest, then stood.

He took a pace forward to stand on the edge of the shade, then held out a hand, inviting them to talk. Accordingly, the guards shoved them forward.

Montgomery said nothing, figuring that he'd let Lomax have the first word, but Lomax must have had the same idea as he kept his mouth clamped shut. Arnold glanced at his men and snorted a laugh that made everyone join in, suggesting that they'd been discussed beforehand.

Dollars changed hands as a bet was decided. Then, with muttered comments and much laughter, further bills were passed around on a new wager after which everyone looked at them eagerly.

Arnold paraded back and forth twice, then swung round to glare at Lomax.

'Where is the gold?' he asked.

'There is no gold,' Lomax said in a calm voice.

Arnold nodded then turned to Montgomery.

'Where is the gold?'

'Lomax wouldn't tell me what he did with it.'

'Yet you were locked inside for a day and your young friend died. How much longer do you need to decide this matter?'

'I will get to the truth,' Montgomery said, even though he judged that Arnold didn't really want an answer to his question.

Sure enough Arnold gestured and the two guards bundled them away. In what had clearly been a pre-arranged plan the rest of Arnold's men moved off. Most of them formed a circle around them while others bustled as they collecting equipment. Montgomery avoided looking at what they were doing, reckoning that it was unlikely to provide any comfort.

'And I haven't got the time to wait,' Arnold said. 'So I'll help you decide the truth now.'

His last comment provided the cue for the men to complete the arrangements, and it rapidly became clear that they were expected to fight.

One man produced Lomax's ornate knife and thrust it into the ground. Then another man kicked out a rough circle with his heel, about forty feet across and with the knife set at the far edge of the circle.

They were pushed inside the circle and a double length of twisted rawhide rope was bound around Montgomery's left wrist. The rope was played out to show that it was nearly as long as the diameter of the circle. The other end was tied to Lomax's left wrist.

Montgomery matched Lomax's confident stance by not struggling and staring at him across the circle. The situation didn't need to be explained.

They were tied together and there was one weapon. Whoever reached that weapon would live.

So Montgomery stood with his feet set wide apart,

his stance relaxed as he prepared to throw himself at the knife when Arnold told them to start. But there was one final twist to the situation.

One man arrived with a three-foot-long wooden stake. He hammered it into the centre of the circle through a loop of the rope, fixing it in place and ensuring both men would have to stay in the circle.

When Montgomery played out the rope he judged that it would fall several feet short of reaching the knife. This ensured that the battle to reach their only weapon would be a difficult one and to get a hand on it he would have to lie on the ground and stretch.

When the stake had been driven a foot into the ground, Arnold came over. The rest of the men stood around the circle. Many held bills aloft and shouted to each other as bets were laid.

'When do we start?' Lomax said, rocking from side to side as he prepared to run for the knife.

'When I give the word,' Arnold said. He paraded around the stake, passing both men and giving them a long stare. 'I will believe whoever lives. If that is Lomax, then I accept there is no gold. If that is Montgomery, then I accept there is gold and I will have it.'

Lomax smirked as Arnold gave Montgomery a no-win situation.

Then Arnold backed away to the edge of the circle, moving out of Montgomery's eyeline. Lomax kept his gaze on Arnold. Montgomery was starting to move to bring him back into view when he caught the flickering in Lomax's gaze that said the signal had been given.

Lomax ran for the knife, pounding his feet to the ground so hard he threw up puffs of dust. Montgomery ran for it too, but he was a half-pace behind him.

Lomax ran seven long paces, then threw himself to the ground, skidding on his belly as he reached for the knife. The rope went taut, dragging him to a halt two feet from the knife. Lomax being left spread-eagled, Montgomery found that he was in the better position.

He ignored the knife and instead dropped down on Lomax's back pinning him to the ground. Lomax tried to buck him, but his being splayed out on the ground and constrained at the extent of his reach meant that he couldn't get the leverage. The attempt failed.

Montgomery reached over his body for the knife. He had the same problem as Lomax had had: that the knife would remain out of reach unless he stretched himself to the utmost.

Montgomery inched his fingers closer, but this moved most of his body off Lomax and gave Lomax the opportunity to thrust an elbow up into Montgomery's chest. The force blasted the air from Montgomery's chest and made him drag his arm in.

He found himself being rolled away as Lomax took advantage of his winded state. Montgomery twisted, then wrapped his arms around Lomax's chest to stop him going for the knife. The two men went tumbling over each other towards the stake, eventually fetching up beside it with Lomax lying on top of Montgomery.

Lomax raised himself, then crashed down a flat-handed blow to Montgomery's cheek. It hammered his head back into the ground with a jarring thud that rattled his teeth. He lay poleaxed with his ears ringing and his limbs splayed, but the lure of the knife proved to be too great and Lomax didn't take advantage of his vulnerable position.

He rolled off Montgomery, then hurried across the circle, his progress gathering a murmur of interest from the watching circle of men.

Montgomery sat up, shaking his head as he struggled to regain his senses. He saw that he was already too late to stop Lomax getting to the knife. Lomax dropped to his knees, then lay on his side with his left arm outstretched to the extent of his reach.

Preparing to defend himself Montgomery stood and settled his stance, then he smiled when he saw Lomax's predicament.

In what had probably been a cruel joke the knife had been driven into the ground at a point that was just too far to reach. Even at the fullest extent of his reach Lomax could only claw at the ground, his fingertips coming down a foot short.

Montgomery looked up and caught Arnold's eye. Arnold returned a smirk that confirmed that this had indeed fact been deliberate. Then Montgomery paced across the circle, the ringing in his ears fading as he shook himself and regained his senses.

This time he didn't jump on Lomax's back but stood over him. When Lomax withdrew his arm to consider an alternative tactic he saw the shadow on the ground and looked up.

Montgomery kicked out. The toe of his boot slammed squarely into Lomax's chin and sent him reeling. He rolled on to his back with his limbs spread wide after his unsuccessful attempt to reach the knife.

Lomax being too stunned to fight back, Montgomery reached down, grabbed his collar and hoisted him to his feet. Then he threw his weight behind a pile-driving punch that sent Lomax staggering away.

After three uncertain paces he righted himself, but Montgomery hurried after him and thundered a low blow into his belly, which bent him double. A backhanded swipe cracked his head back and stood him upright before Montgomery kicked his feet from under him, sending him heavily to the ground.

Montgomery didn't give him a chance to recover. Again he dragged Lomax to his feet, then rolled his shoulders and scythed a blow into Lomax's cheek that sent him reeling.

Lomax staggered away for several paces until he walked into the stake that was keeping them tethered within the circle. He made to grab it to hold himself up, but his strength gave way and he slipped down to sit on the ground clutching the stake.

Montgomery considered him and his bowed form, then looked around the circle of watchers. Money was changing hands as the likely victor became more apparent. This sight decided it for Montgomery.

For twenty years he'd shared Wallace's and Jack's obsession: to one day track down Lomax Rhinehart and make him pay for what he'd done in the last days of the war. If he and Lomax were alone, he'd have had no compunction about ending their fight, but he had no desire to kill a man so that others could win a bet.

He turned on the spot, hoping to catch the eye of someone who didn't share his enthusiasm for this blood sport. Nobody met his gaze although many shouted at him to end it while he could.

He ended his consideration facing the knife, then looked up to Arnold Hays, who had moved round to stand behind it.

Arnold looked down at the knife then up to Montgomery.

'Kill him and you live,' he said. 'I know there's no gold. A snivelling little runt like Lomax Rhinehart would never have got his hands on twenty gold bars.'

The offer didn't cheer Montgomery, but he also didn't see that he had a choice. He took slow paces forward to reach the limit of his range, then bent down. With one hand stretched forward he reached for the knife.

He wondered whether Arnold would kick it over

so that he could palm it. Arnold didn't, but to his surprise he was able to move his hand closer and closer to the knife, getting to within inches before he was pulled up.

He was taller than Lomax, and the man who had driven the stake in hadn't been precise in positioning the rope in the exact centre of the circle. So it was possible that the knife had always been within his reach, but not Lomax's.

He knelt, then stretched. This time his fingertips brushed the hilt. He flexed his muscles, then tried again, managing to press a fingertip to the knife, then a whole finger.

He continued to stretch. Then, in a moment, his straining let him lunge forward and he easily wrapped several fingers around the knife. Arnold chuckled and Montgomery looked up, but Arnold wasn't watching him. He was looking beyond him.

The thought came that since the stake was constraining him perhaps he shouldn't have been able to reach the knife, after all. That thought saved his life as he whipped back his arm and rolled over on to his side.

The stake came crashing down into the ground where his head had been a moment earlier.

Lomax had given up trying to reach the knife. Instead he had wrested free the only other weapon available to him: the stake that kept them within the circle. He looked up to see Lomax raise the stake high above his head ready for a more accurate pulverizing blow.

In desperation Montgomery kicked out. The sole of his boot slammed into Lomax's shin and sent him to one knee as he brought the stake down. Lomax's ill-directed blow drove the stake into the ground a foot from Montgomery's shoulder and unbalanced Lomax so that he fell forward to land on top of him.

Montgomery tried to buck him away, but Lomax settled his weight on him. Then, with a great roar, he put both hands to the stake and tore it from the ground. He held it sideways above Montgomery's head. Then he bore down.

Montgomery thrust up both hands and caught the stake, stopping it a foot above his head. Then, with his elbows planted firmly to the ground, he held it steady.

Lomax strained and moved himself up Montgomery's body to get better leverage. Using his full weight he pushed down, gradually driving the stake lower. Montgomery's elbows splayed as the stake moved inexorably closer to his head.

He didn't think he could slow its progress, so he tried to kick Lomax away. But Lomax had settled his weight in a position from which he couldn't easily be dislodged. Montgomery jerked his head to the side searching for the knife, which must be close by, but it wasn't visible.

He looked further afield. To his surprise he saw that many of the men were no longer watching their fight. There were gaps in the circle and several men were walking away.

A sudden surge of anger gave Montgomery renewed strength, finding that fighting for these men's entertainment wasn't as annoying as their not being interested.

He stayed the progress of the stake, then even managed to raise it, but that progress encouraged Lomax to flex his shoulders. He shoved down.

This time Montgomery couldn't slow the stake and, worse, it was moving towards his throat. The wood touched his neck, then pressed in.

To give himself leeway Montgomery rolled his head to the side. The wood still pressed in, making him gasp, but he could also see what was interesting the men.

A cavalcade of riders was coming into the fort. Elizabeth and Dean were up front. Behind them rode Herman.

Montgomery didn't know what had been happening back in Sunrise while they'd been incarcerated, but it was a reasonable guess that Arnold had resolved to carry through his threat and round up some replacement townsfolk to kill.

Before the descending stake could cut off his windpipe Montgomery grunted with surprise, then looked up at Lomax, trying with his wide-open eyes to signal the change in their circumstances.

His assailant glared down at him with unconcealed bloodlust, but the urgency in Montgomery's gaze must have alerted him. He flinched then looked up.

His eyes opened wide in shock, at least proving that his apparent concern for the fate of the people of Sunrise was genuine, but the sight only encouraged him to redouble his efforts.

With a grunt of anger he pressed down and slowly Montgomery's vision dimmed.

CHAPTER 14

'Kill him and you live,' Arnold said, his voice seeming as if it came from a great distance.

'Tell me what you're doing with them first,' Lomax said, his voice louder and coming from closer to. Then his face came into focus as Montgomery's vision brightened.

'That is to be decided.'

Montgomery gulped, finding that he could breath. He glanced down to see that Lomax had stopped pressing down with the stake, giving him enough leeway to breathe.

He didn't know whether this was deliberate, so he didn't risk alerting Lomax by fighting back. Instead he moved his head slightly.

From the corner of his eye he looked at the gateway. Herman's prisoners were approaching.

'You said I'd live if I killed him,' Lomax said.

'And you will.' Arnold chuckled. 'But I made no promises about the others.'

Lomax's face reddened. His mouth opened and closed as he struggled to find the right words for a retort. Then he tore the stake away from Montgomery's limp grasp and held it aloft one-handed with the sharp end aimed forward.

Then he rolled forward and hurled the stake at Arnold.

Montgomery jerked his head back to follow its progress. Lomax's aim was poor. The stake veered away from Arnold and hammered into the chest of the man to his right. He went down, his hands clawing at the bloodied stake impaling his chest.

Lomax continued his forward motion and leapt at the knife.

Montgomery drew himself up to his knees and groggily prepared to repel his assault, but Lomax, when he had gathered up the knife, ignored him and looked around for the nearest target amongst Arnold's men.

By the gateway the two apparent prisoners had broken away from Herman. Dean rode along beside the fort's wall seeking to outflank Arnold's men, but Elizabeth in a reckless act hurried her horse on towards Lomax.

Luckily the men followed Dean and she approached the circle without anyone turning a gun on her. At a trot, she reached down to help Lomax mount up.

Lomax thrust up a hand, but as he waited for her to reach him he glanced at Montgomery. Then, with an ironic smile on his lips, he underhanded the knife to him.

Montgomery flinched away, but then he saw that the action hadn't been malicious and the knife fell harmlessly at his feet.

As Lomax slipped on to the back of Elizabeth's horse, Montgomery started to raise a hand to acknowledge the act, but then a shadow darkened the ground at his feet.

He dropped to his knees and grabbed the knife, the motion saving him from a lunging blow from behind. Then he rose up while twisting.

At the last moment he confirmed that one of Arnold's men was sneaking up on him. Then the knife dug deep into his assailant's belly.

The two men glared at each other. Then his opponent's eyes glazed and he fell away from the knife. Montgomery wasted no time in tucking the knife into his belt, then rolling the man over to take his gun and gunbelt.

Armed, he took stock of the situation.

Several men had appeared in the fort gateway and were turning guns on Arnold's men. They were too far away for him to discern who they were, but the fact that Herman had dismounted and was running for cover suggested that all was not as it seemed.

Elizabeth and Dean weren't Herman's prisoners; he was theirs. And that meant that the townsfolk had at last decided to take on Arnold.

Their unexpected arrival had already sown confusion amongst Arnold and his men. Most of them were hurrying to the armoury to make a stand. Some men headed round the corner and out of view while others dived behind a heaped pile of lumber. Three men were heading to the gateway to repel the new arrivals.

Montgomery looked for Lomax and Elizabeth. He saw them jump down from their horses and hurry into cover behind an upturned buggy that stood square on to the armoury.

As Dean was veering away from the wall to join them, Montgomery decided this was a sensible move. With his head down he hurried away from the circle. He pounded across the ground, gritting his teeth at every pace in the expectation of being shot in the back, but without reprisals he was able to run behind the wagon to join the line of people hiding there.

'Where's Nick?' he asked.

Dean pointed to a position twenty yards from the gateway.

'While we came in with Herman,' he said, 'he stayed with the rest of the townsfolk. Some are in the gateway while the rest are taking up positions behind the stockade. They'll be gunning for Arnold at any moment.'

Lomax moved over to join them. He slapped Dean on the shoulder.

'Then we need to make sure they succeed,' he said. He pointed at the porch outside the officers' quarters, which Arnold had now abandoned. 'That means we need to spread out.'

Dean nodded. Lomax glanced at Montgomery and smirked, acknowledging the sudden turn of events that had curtailed their attempts to kill each other.

Although Montgomery wasn't enthused about letting Lomax give the orders, he had to admit he'd had the right idea of avoiding being pinned down.

'I'll cover you,' he said.

Dean and Lomax nodded. Then, on the count of three, they hurried out from the wagon bent double. Montgomery stayed his fire until two of Arnold's men noticed their flight and raised themselves from behind the pile of lumber. Then he laid down a burst of gunfire that forced them to dive for cover.

Lomax and Dean hurried into the porch where they took cover behind a table in the doorway. Arnold's men risked blasting a volley of lead at them, but when Montgomery returned fire they ducked. Then slowly they spread out to array their forces in positions that mainly faced the gateway.

While keeping down behind the wagon, Elizabeth cast Montgomery a quick glance.

'I'm sorry about what happened to you,' she said. 'I really had planned to defeat Arnold.'

'I know.' He glanced at the townsfolk lurking in the gateway. 'And I'm pleased you've done the right thing at last, even if it is too late for Wallace Sheckley.'

Elizabeth winced. 'Lomax hated what he was

forced to do. I'm sure it was the same for Pike and Snyder.'

Montgomery wondered whether he should retort, but her answer sounded honest, suggesting that most people didn't know exactly what had been happening at the outcrop.

'How did you meet Lomax?' he asked.

Elizabeth turned away from her studious consideration of the armoury through a gap in the wood to consider him.

'That's an odd question.'

Montgomery shrugged. 'My time with Arnold Hays followed by Nick's escape has been odd.'

Although he hadn't answered her question, she replied quickly.

'Lomax arrived in town a year ago. When my husband disappeared, he was good to me. We've become close.'

That summary was light on details, but Montgomery could fill in the gaps for himself and that meant he hadn't misinterpreted Lomax's motives nor his recent change of heart.

Despite this, he still offered a reassuring smile, but before he could reply gunfire exploded from the gateway.

He raised himself. Two of the three men who had moved closer to the gateway were lying on the ground with blooming gunshot wounds staining their backs.

The third man was beating a hasty retreat across

the quadrangle. He hadn't got far when a shot to the back sent him tumbling.

Then the townsfolk appeared on either side of the gateway, peering over the stockade.

On the porch Lomax raised himself and waved at the armoury. As several men acknowledged the instruction, Montgomery caught a glimpse of Nick to the right of the gateway. Then the townsfolk laid down a burst of gunfire, forcing Arnold and his dozen or so men to keep down.

For the next ten minutes the groups traded lead, but with Arnold's men having such good cover beside the armoury and behind the lumber pile the townsfolk made no further headway.

Montgomery reckoned Arnold could remain holed up for as long as he wanted to and the townsfolk would have to take all the risks in crossing the open square to reach him.

Lomax must have had the same thought as he edged out from the porch. Then, with Dean covering him, he ran to the closest available cover before the armoury, a pile of rubble twenty feet away. He threw himself on to his belly. Then over the top he fired at Arnold's men.

With Lomax and Montgomery covering him, Dean moved to join Lomax. He had covered half the distance when Arnold's men got themselves organized. A volley of gunshots peppered across the ground at his feet and forced him to backtrack.

Dean ran back to the porch, but he'd managed

only a few paces when repeated gunshots ripped into his back and sent him to his knees then to lie flat. Then Arnold barked out orders and two men moved out while keeping low, aiming to outflank Lomax.

Montgomery took a pot shot at one man, forcing him to drop from view. Then he swung his gun to the side to shoot at the second man, but he dived to safety before Montgomery could fire.

Despite the success Montgomery shook his head.

'Lomax is doomed,' he said, 'unless he can get back to the porch.'

'Then you have to help him,' Elizabeth said, distress making her voice high-pitched.

After two decades of wanting to kill Lomax and several attempts in the last day by each of them to kill the other, Montgomery was minded to snap back a retort.

One look at Elizabeth's imploring wide-eyed expression persuaded him that defeating Arnold Hays was the main objective here. Lomax's fate could wait.

'All right,' he said. 'But no matter what happens next, stay here.'

CHAPTER 15

As gunfire blasted behind him, Montgomery set off along the back of the wagon to the corner, where he considered the situation.

He judged that the townsfolk by the gate would keep Arnold from venturing too far away from the armoury. But approaching them as Lomax had done would be risky.

So, after giving Elizabeth a last comforting smile, he turned on his heel and ran away from the wagon. He ran on a route that kept it between him and Arnold to cover his actions.

Thirty yards away he veered to the side and ran behind the officers' quarters. He was unsure of the layout of the fort, but he had some luck when he reached the back and saw that a route was available that would let him get to the armoury.

He hurried past the building and reached the armoury's back wall without being seen. From his new position he could still hear gunfire ripping out on the main quadrangle, but he judged that it was mainly Arnold and the townsfolk trading speculative shots.

He could try to sneak up on Arnold's men by heading along the side of the building, but the moment they saw him approaching he would be trapped on open ground.

He looked up. Last night he had been unable to climb the smooth stone inside the building, but the outside was weathered and provided many footholds.

He holstered his gun and climbed.

Without too much difficulty he clambered up the back wall in a minute, then rolled on to the flat roof. Halfway along was the gap through which Nick had escaped. From his elevated position he had a good view of the fort.

Nick and James were now amongst the group in the gateway. Nick was shooting with steady determination while James was giving the townsfolk orders to spread out along the wall.

Montgomery reckoned that if they were aiming to launch an assault on Arnold this would be the decisive moment in the battle. So he hurried to the front of the building and peered down.

Below, Arnold's men were splayed out behind the piled-up lumber and they were all in hidden positions. But their positions were only effective to repel the assault from the gateway or from Lomax's position. They didn't expect that someone would sneak up on them from behind.

Montgomery made them pay for that oversight when he dispatched the two men nearest to Lomax with shots to the back.

Then before he could be spotted he ducked back down. Grunts of consternation arose from below followed by frantic gunfire, but none of it was aimed in his direction.

He waited until it petered out, then bobbed up and picked off the next two men behind the lumber. This time several of the men saw him and with quick reflexes they swung round to lie on their backs and pepper lead up at him.

Bullets kicked shards off the stone rim of the roof and forced him to back away out of sight, where he remained until the firing petered out. Then he risked moving forward again, but now they'd got him in their sights and a rapid volley blasted out that whistled around his head.

He jerked backwards without firing. On his knees he crawled to the middle of the roof and raised himself. Again, gunfire tore out as the men below quickly picked out his new position.

One slug bit into the rim so close that a stone shard tore across his forearm. Sharp pain made him flinch back then flex his arm to check that it was only scratched.

When he looked up the situation was changing. Even if he couldn't continue to pick off the men below, the distraction had encouraged the townsfolk to risk coming out from the gateway, firing on the run. Lomax joined them in blasting slugs at the armoury.

Montgomery raised himself as much as was possible without being seen from below. He saw that two men were trying to outflank Lomax by slowly snaking along the ground towards his position.

Lomax must have heard them coming, as he bobbed up to fire at them. He dispatched the left-hand man with his first shot and this panicked the second man into jumping to his feet, then dashing towards him. He fired on the run, the lead winging off the rubble.

Lomax jumped up and met his onslaught with a deadly shot that tore into the man's belly. The man ran on for two paces before keeling over to land at Lomax's feet.

Then, seeing the numerous bodies that showed they now had the ascendancy, Lomax made the reckless move of charging at Arnold's position. When Montgomery saw that everyone's attention was on Lomax, he jumped up to aid him.

As Lomax pounded across the ground, Montgomery dispatched one man, then another with deadly shots to the back.

In five long strides Lomax reached the corner of the armoury. Montgomery's intervention had sowed enough panic to ensure he didn't get any accurate retaliation. Then Arnold's remaining men got themselves organized and a solid phalanx of weaponry turned on him.

Lomax picked out Arnold and fired, the shot whistling over his shoulder. Then an instinct for self-preservation overcame his bravado and he scurried along the armoury wall with his head down. Slugs tore into the wall behind his back before he dived for the armoury door.

He hit the ground a few feet short of his objective then rolled through the open doorway as gunfire clattered into the stone.

When he had disappeared from view the gun-slingers turned to Montgomery. Only four men were left, but they swung their guns upwards with grim efficiency. Montgomery was about to dive flat, but then he saw that Arnold was running doubled-over for the doorway.

Montgomery glanced down to check where the door was, then dropped from view. Gunfire clattered along the roof as, with his head down, he moved three yards to his left. He listened to Arnold's pattering feet below, then leaned over the roof and aimed down.

Arnold was running towards him, but his fore-shortened figure presented only a small target and Montgomery's shot clattered feet wide. Then, in a sudden decision, Montgomery climbed on to the rim and leapt from the roof.

At the last moment Arnold saw him dropping down. He glanced up, but he was too late. Montgomery slammed on to his back, flattening him. Montgomery lay for a moment, his limbs entangled with Arnold's, before he scrambled to his feet.

Arnold's men had followed his progress and were training their guns on him, so he had no choice but to follow Lomax in diving through the door. He rolled, then came up on his feet and looked round for Arnold.

He didn't have to look far.

Arnold was getting to his feet, aiming to follow him in, but he was still winded and he was moving slowly.

Montgomery made him pay for his slowness when with a fluid motion he raised his gun and fired. His single shot caught Arnold high in the chest and sent him rocking back into the side of the doorway, his mouth opening in surprise.

Then a second shot came from behind Montgomery. It hit Arnold squarely between the eyes, making him slide down the door then topple over to lie in a crumpled heap outside.

Montgomery jerked round, placed his back to the wall and peered into the darkness. In the gloom he could see Lomax's outline ten feet away, his gun drawn and aimed through the doorway, waiting for whoever dared to come in next.

'So,' Montgomery said, 'it seems we're fighting on the same side, after all.'

'We are,' Lomax said, his tone light, 'but that won't be for long. With Arnold killed, the few who remain will crumble.'

'They will, and then we can sort out our problems.'

153

'There's no need for that.' Lomax flashed a smile. 'You should trust me.'

'Never.' Montgomery returned the smile. 'I know why those other set of bones is out on the outcrop.'

Lomax lowered his head for a moment.

'You worked that out, but you don't know the full story.' Lomax lowered his voice. 'Elizabeth's husband was an evil man.'

'You always have an excuse for your actions: the raiders we captured deserved their fate. You were saving the lives of the Sunrise townsfolk when you killed Wallace. And now you say you were helping Elizabeth by killing her husband. Why not stop the lies and admit the truth that you're a cold-hearted killer who enjoys inflicting pain?'

'I can't.' Lomax shrugged. 'Because that's not the way it is.'

Keeping his gun trained on the doorway he moved towards it. From outside fierce gunfire was exploding out across the square, presumably as the townsfolk mounted their assault on the armoury.

Lomax winced, then craned his neck to look through the doorway at something outside. That made Montgomery turn to see what was happening. But at that moment Lomax jerked his gun to the side, the weapon arcing round to aim at Montgomery's chest.

He was too slow.

With his gaze set on the doorway Montgomery fired. His low shot to the side bent Lomax double.

154

Lomax looked up, a hand clutched to his guts, his wide eyes registering his surprise that Montgomery had managed to shoot him.

He snorted a laugh. 'So it seems I'll get a quick end, not like Wallace who begged and whined until—'

Montgomery fired again, this time hitting him high in the chest and sending him rolling to lie on his back. With his gun still trained down on his chest he paced across the armoury to stand over him.

'The speed doesn't matter none,' he said. 'You've finally got what you deserved.'

Lomax gasped and arched his back. When he flopped down he was breathing shallowly.

'Do one thing for me, please,' he whispered, his voice fading fast. 'Don't tell her about me. Let her memories of me be good ones.'

Montgomery was minded to refuse, but Lomax's tone had conveyed genuine concern. As Lomax relaxed and his gun fell from his grasp, he nodded.

'I promise.' He waited until Lomax gave a weak smile, then loomed over him as Lomax would have done to Wallace and the others he'd killed. 'But I'll do it for her. She shouldn't have to live with knowing what an evil man you were.'

Lomax curled his lip in a sneer, struggling to summon the strength to reply as Montgomery drew Lomax's ornate knife from his belt. He held it up to the light to make sure that Lomax could see it. Then, with a contemptuous flick of the wrist, he slammed it down. The knife buried itself up to the hilt in Lomax's chest.

Montgomery stood over him as he breathed his last, remembering Wallace, the bones at the outcrop, the others twenty years ago. Then he headed to the doorway and looked out.

He had been right about the situation. With Arnold dead, his few remaining men had panicked. Most of them were running across the square to the stables aiming to reach their horses to flee the fort.

The townsfolk were making them pay dearly for every frantic yard they scrambled.

After a last glance at Lomax's still form, Montgomery headed out of the armoury, aiming to add to their woes.

CHAPTER 16

'Should I write anything on this one?' Nick asked, standing back.

Montgomery also stood back, judging that this wasn't a matter for him to decide.

Now that Arnold Hays had been defeated remorse for their actions had overcome the townsfolk. A dozen people had headed out to the outcrop to give a proper burial to Wallace and the other victim.

The sight they'd found there had shocked everyone and, in a sombre mood, they'd buried the bodies. But after much consultation the man who had died a mile away from the scene of the atrocity remained unidentified.

'Leave it blank,' Elizabeth said.

She had a pensive stare as she looked at this man's grave.

Montgomery had told her that Lomax had died at Arnold's hands in the armoury. Afterwards he had kept his promise, but what she had seen here had shocked her and it must have started her thinking.

Montgomery nodded. 'Perhaps one day someone will come looking for him and provide a name.'

She nodded. So, with the grim task complete, the townsfolk got ready to return. As Montgomery and Nick weren't returning to Sunrise, the townsfolk lined up to thank them. Most couldn't meet their eyes. Only Elizabeth dallied to talk. She glanced at the last grave.

'Do you reckon there's any chance he's. . . ?' Her voice trailed off and she lowered her head, unwilling to voice the thought.

'I don't know,' Montgomery said, 'but perhaps you could pretend it is your husband. You don't have a grave to mark his passing, so you could come here from time to time to pay your respects and to think. Maybe that'll help you work it out.'

'I'll do that.' She moved to leave, but then turned back. 'Will you ever visit Sunrise again?'

'Maybe,' Montgomery said, then favoured her with a smile that made her nod before she joined the others in leaving.

Montgomery and Nick watched the townsfolk mount up. Neither man moved until they had reached the trail. Then they took a slow walk to Wallace's grave where they paused for a minute in silent thought before they headed to their horses.

'If she keeps coming back here,' Nick said when they'd mounted up, 'she's sure one day to head along the outcrop and find the stakes that Lomax used to pin out her husband. She'll work it out.'

'I know. But that'll mean I kept my promise, and it'll let her work it out when she's ready to accept the truth.'

'And after that, will you come back here to see her again?'

Montgomery laughed. 'That's something I'd have talked about with Wallace and your father, but no matter how much you've impressed me, I won't be talking about it with you.'

Nick shrugged. 'Then maybe you should come back home with me so you can talk to my father about it.'

Montgomery raised the reins, but then lowered them as he considered.

'Now that's a mighty fine idea.' Montgomery gestured ahead for Nick to lead on. 'And on the way maybe I can tell you some tales about your father.'

'I'd like that too,' Nick said, smiling.